WHAT DID THE OLD LADY KNOW?

Hannah Maslin nodded her head at her strategic curtain.

"People would be surprised at what I can see from my little corner."

"I'm sure they would. And what did you see yesterday evening?"

"I saw what I saw."

"Mrs. Maslin—"

"I can't tell you who it was, because I don't know. I saw the schoolmaster on his bike. I've felt sorry for him all along, though things would have been different if he'd acted differently. Everything that's happened, he's brought on to himself. He should have stuck to the old ways of doing things. But he was no match for those girls. Wicked girls."

"Why do you call them wicked?"

"Because I see what I see . . ."

LESSON IN MURDER

JOHN BUXTON HILTON

Originally published as *The Innocents at Home*

DIAMOND BOOKS, NEW YORK

This Diamond book contains the complete
text of the original hardcover edition.
It has been completely reset in a typeface
designed for easy reading and was printed
from new film.

This book was originally
published in Great Britain
as *The Innocents at Home*.

LESSON IN MURDER

A Diamond Book / published by arrangement with
the author's estate

PRINTING HISTORY
William Collins Sons & Co. edition published in 1986
St. Martin's Press edition published in 1987
Diamond edition / October 1991

ISBN: 1-55773-602-2

Diamond Books are published by The Berkley Publishing Group,
200 Madison Avenue, New York, New York 10016.
The name "DIAMOND" and its logo are trademarks
belonging to Charter Communications, Inc.

PRINTED IN THE UNITED STATES OF AMERICA

10 9 8 7 6 5 4 3 2 1

LESSON IN MURDER

• 1 •

By THE TIME Kenworthy was a Chief Inspector, it was becoming less common for Chief Constables to feel they had to call in the Met. But it still happened sometimes. Sometimes there were political undertones. Sometimes the Chief did not feel as sure as he ought to have been of his head of CID. Sometimes he knew his team was riven by incompatibilities and jealousies that should have been beneath mature men and women. Sometimes he knew that the dragnet needed to be wider-ranging than he could manage.

The last time that Kenworthy was sent Cook's-touring in the provinces, the scene had a very local look about it. His winger was Sergeant Parrott, whom he had still to get to know. The venue was a weather-bashed sector of the Fenlands, at a season of the year when the climate could be misery. His county oppos briefed him meticulously—but he was left to guess why Norfolk felt they needed him.

As always, a lot had happened before he made his entrance . . .

Linda Calvert tried to keep the image of Hannah Maslin out of her mind: her bristly chin, her sagging flour-sack of bosom. In the normal run of life she would have crossed the road with her baby-buggy rather than come face to face with the old woman. There was something about Hannah Maslin that was revoltingly anti-feminine, one might almost say deliberately, aggressively anti-human. For one thing she was grossly overweight—though outsize women were hardly an exception at King's Lynn's Tuesday Market. She would have turned the weighing machine, if she had ever stood on one, at twenty-two stone. And she smelled (according to those unfortunates who had from time to time been compelled to sit beside her on the Tuesday bus) of a lifetime of body-odours absorbed into layer upon layer of antediluvian underwear. Hannah Maslin flaunted her anti-humanity as if it were the only weapon with which she could punish the rest of the world for being human.

Tales were told about Hannah Maslin that must surely be making the most of the truth—though roughly the same stories did have the habit of turning up from different quarters. She had led, it was said, a youth of insatiable and wide-ranging immorality. And that triggered off a series of obscene images, for her looks must always have been disgusting, and her physical frame could never have been normal. But the last to learn of her reputation had been William Maslin, plasterer, who had hanged himself from the bough of an apple-tree after seven years of trying to be married to her.

Hannah Maslin never made open warfare in the village. Perhaps with some of the older inhabitants she would not have dared, though that did not mean that she had any respect for them. Her contempt for the younger families was abysmal—and they accounted nowadays for something like two-thirds of the population. She rarely mounted a frontal attack, but her loud mutterings to herself were a terrifying substitute, leaving no doubt about her hatred of anything new and, most particularly, of anyone who looked or sounded self-satisfied.

There was only one aspect of life in which Hannah Maslin was rumoured to be approachable, and Linda Calvert was driven by despair—as must surely have been anyone else who had ever voluntarily trodden the crumbling brick path through the old woman's derelict garden.

Hannah Maslin lived in one of the few cottages in St. Botolph's Fen End that still retained the look of the old village. It was built in an ancient, mellowed, orange-coloured brick and looked tall—though that was only because it was narrow. St. Botolph's Fen End had once been a shapeless assembly of such cottages, scanning the surrounding reclaimed marshes as if they were the deckhouses of phantom ships. Now almost every one had been rendered, Snow-cemmed and re-roofed, their leaded lights replaced by glaring expanses of picture window. The older generation had either found their way to hospitals and nursing-homes to die, or been rehoused in the parabola of semi-detached council houses in School Close. Nearly all the older properties had changed hands at figures that made a fantasy of the prices for which they had been built. They had been gutted and revamped and now housed North Sea oil rig widows, executives from the industrial estates of North-West Norfolk and even an obstinate case or two of London commuter.

Linda Calvert's friends had warned her that Hannah Maslin's front door had been disused for so long that its bolts were wedged solid. Besides, to knock on it might be to suggest that you considered yourself socially distinguished enough to have her open it for you, at which Hannah might take raucous offence. Linda Calvert therefore went along the path that ran up the side of the house, flanked on the left by wet and out-reaching brambles that clawed at Gemma in the buggy, and on the right by such articles of bygone domesticity as the old woman had jettisoned over the years: a mangle with wooden rollers rotted through; a decomposing rubber enema; the frame, without wheels or handlebars, of a cheap bicycle of the nineteen-thirties.

At the back of the house was a shed whose door stood partially open to reveal a decrepit deal table loaded with tins, jars and broken-handled teacups. Was it in there that the old woman made up her concoctions? In a less permissive age had women come to her for vile brews that could destroy their injudiciously conceived embryos—and put their own lives in jeopardy? Linda Calvert could not think of Hannah Maslin without tapping new seams of nausea. She had only forced herself to come here because Jenny Young had been so impressed by the old rat-bag. Jenny had not claimed that Hannah had cured her psoriasis, but she swore that the patches on her legs had diminished to a quarter of their size after a week of her ointment. That was after years of failure by doctors, chemists, and homeopathists alike. And no one could have called Jenny unfussy.

Linda was tempted to turn on her heel, but in spite of her revulsion she knocked—because Mrs. Maslin was watching her from her living-room, and though she did not come to the door, she was likely to rush out, bawling abuse, if Linda turned away. She was an irrational woman who might at any moment interpret some nuance of behaviour as an insult.

Even when Linda knocked, Mrs. Maslin did not answer at once. She came first to look out of the window and then vanished into her household shadows as if what she had seen had dispelled any interest she might have had in her caller. With a kind of relief, Linda was about to push the buggy back down the path. But then the sticking door was pulled open with a creak and Hannah Maslin was standing a foot away from her, as if shamelessly boasting of what a revolting object the mortal frame could become.

"Yes?"

"I wonder if I could ask for your help?"

"Everybody wants old Hannah's help," the crone said, addressing herself not so much to Linda as to some unseen circle of familiars. "And what sort of help do you think I'm likely to be to you? Are you collecting for charity?"

"No, no."

She felt the familiar tightening in her chest.

"Asthma," she said. "It's got worse since I came here—"

The old woman was standing, bulky and bristled, in such a way that Linda could not see beyond her into the house. Linda wanted to back away, but she knew that this would be construed as the culmination of all insults.

"You should have stayed where you came from. The marshes are too low-lying for you."

"We have to live where my husband's work is. And I like it very much here."

Perhaps it was a good move to say something in praise of East Anglia.

"And you've done so much good to one of my friends."

"What have you tried?"

"I've been to the doctor, but I can't seem to get him interested. He seems to think it's something I've just got to put up with."

"You'd better come in."

The room was overheated. Its atmosphere hit her like a wave. And it was only when she was inside that she saw that Hannah had another visitor. Sitting on a corner of the worn-down sofa, a small pile of magazines from the 1920s on her lap, was Davina Norris, looking across at her with what she could only describe by the paradox of expressionless insolence.

There was in the room an overriding smell of which it was impossible to distinguish individual ingredients. The dominant aroma—cinnamon, nutmeg, oil of cloves?—was not what one expected to meet in a village slum. The furniture was mostly unmatched pieces that might originally have been gathered together by Hannah's impoverished grandmother. The pictures on her walls, none more recent than Edwardian, were mostly sentimental, faded and ravaged by damp. In the front window there hung a rolling pin of Bristol blue glass, an antique and the only object in sight that might be worth a few pounds.

Davina Norris gave no sign at all that she recognized Linda. It was true that they had never had anything direct to do with each other. Did the child consider herself so damned superior? It was said that she had a brain that made IQ history. Linda was in no position to judge. There had been this appalling business with Henry Gower, and although no one could understand what had got into the man, for whom there could be no possible excuse, no one believed that Davina and her friends were entirely blameless. No one of Linda's acquaintance believed that, anyway.

And what was this upmarket, pampered twelve-year-old doing here with Hannah Maslin? It staggered Linda that there was any liaison between them, and yet the child was sitting in her corner, saying nothing, as if she was certainly no stranger to the room.

Hannah Maslin went to a cupboard. Everybody said her saving grace was that the moment she turned her attention to herbs, she became a different person, single-minded, sympathetic. One might almost say there was something professional about her, if you could use that word of anyone so gross. It would have been too much to call this side of her life hygienic, but she handled her brews and powders with obvious respect for them, and she clearly made some effort to keep the jars and old tea-caddies on her shelves reasonably tidy. She opened a drawer and brought out a packet of conical paper bags. They looked surprisingly clean; she must have bought them years ago in expectation of regular retail trade. She filled one of them from a battered canister.

"Make the most of this. When it's all gone, I don't know where the next lot's coming from. I don't get about as I did and I can't bend to my plot any more. If you want it to do you any good, you'll have to persevere."

"I'll persevere with anything that might rid me of this pestilence."

"Brew it three times a day, as if you were making tea, two spoons to the pot. It will do you no harm to chew it between your teeth between meals. And whatever's left in your cup, snuff it up your nose: keep your tubes clear. But I suppose you're too finicky to do that—"

On the sofa, the child sniggered, nastily. Hannah turned and barked at her.

"I'll not have you here if you don't know how to behave."

The child shrugged her shoulders impudently.

"Go on, then—out with you."

Davina Norris got up with provocative sloth and left the cottage, leaving the door slightly ajar behind her.

"I'm prepared to try anything," Linda said.

But Hannah Maslin's interest in Linda Calvert seemed to have evaporated. As she crossed to close the door, she caught sight of something or someone out in the village street. From where she was standing, Linda could not see who or what it was, but Mrs. Maslin's habit of talking to herself provided limited information.

"Why, the lard-headed fool!"

She was so infuriated by what she saw that she went up to her window corner and drew back the curtain. It was a wonder that the curtain had not developed a permanent crease, so often had the village seen it withdrawn that vital inch.

She stared out for long seconds, then came waddling back across the room, handing Linda the bag.

"How much do I owe you for this, Mrs. Maslin?"

"I always say people should give what they think it's worth to them," old Hannah said, perhaps hinting that as Linda's husband travelled to London three times a week, she could afford to pay above the odds. Linda gave her a fifty-pence piece, the price that Jenny Young had told her she had paid. The old woman accepted it with signs of neither dissatisfaction nor disgust.

Linda let herself out of the cottage and the air struck keen and sweet. She looked up and down the street, but at first could see nothing that might have attracted Hannah Maslin's attention. There was nothing in the afternoon life of St. Botolph's Fen End that seemed worthy of curiosity. A knot of mothers was coming away from the playground gate having collected their offspring from the school. There was a television van from Lynn outside the Masons'—servicing or repossessing. Jenny Young was coming out of the shop with a packet of breakfast cereal.

And then she saw that Henry Gower himself was loitering further down the road. He was watching the children strung across the school yard—very few of the older ones were being met—and, spotting a particular child, he moved across the road in a wide arc to waylay her.

It was Elsie Frost, peaky and pale. When she saw Henry

Gower coming towards her, she let out an undisciplined scream and ran. Every mother at the gate turned to look.

Henry Gower stepped back, making it clear that he was making no further effort to approach the child. He looked round the other children. You could see that the next to catch his eye was fat Pauline Dean. Pauline turned on her heel and put a group of mums between herself and Gower.

Linda crossed the road to show Jenny her precious booty from the Maslin cupboard.

"My God!" Jenny said.

Linda thought at first that her surprise had something to do with the herbal mixture. But Jenny was looking down the road. "That fool Henry Gower is going down Mill Lane with Davina Norris. In full view of half the village. You'd think he'd have more sense. They can call it interfering with a witness. That's just about all he needs."

• 2 •

THEY HAD MADE a book in the CID room on Henry Gower's chances and the odds against an acquittal had stabilized at six to four. It was when it came to side-bets on his sentence that some of the more subtle flavours of the case came into play.

"Swingeing fine," was Detective-Constable Warburton's forecast. He was not claiming to guess the temper of the court, but was influenced by his assessment of moral as against legal guilt.

"When you think of what he's going to lose along the line—his job, his pension and his house—"

"Fair enough too," Detective-Sergeant Harrold said. "How would you feel if one of them had been your kid?"

"I'm not convinced that he did them all that much harm."

"Not ours to say, Dicky. How are you to know what goes on in a kid's mind?"

"Didn't you ever exercise your vulgar curiosity with little girls behind the bogs when you were a youngster, Sarge?"

"That's not the same thing as filth and interference by an adult—and one supposed to be in authority. What if they were to find him guilty and put him on probation? Would you still want him teaching any kid of yours?"

"That'll not happen anyway. The public wouldn't wear it. Look, Sarge—I'm not condoning what he did. He's been bloody stupid, and a man in his position has no right to be stupid. We have the right to expect a man in public office to show judgement. But I still don't think he did that much harm. The harm only started happening when we moved in."

"You're in a bloody liberal-minded mood this morning, Dicky."

WPC Price spoke up.

"I've said all along, it's not only the harm he did them we should be thinking about. It's the harm they've done him."

"Now watch it, Patsy," the Sergeant told her. "You already had it in the neck from Connie for saying just that."

"I did. And I still think it's true, so I'm saying it again. But I'll know better another time than to put it down on paper."

One sentence in her First Supplementary Crime Report: Connie had seized on it like a kitten pouncing on a beetle.

"This is not the place for moral opinions or amateur psychology, Price. Those things are neither your concern nor mine. Confine yourself to facts, evidence and the law."

A bad mark for Patsy Price. She felt as if her reputation had gone back to that of a square one recruit. Chances for Connie to look directly over one's shoulder were mercifully rare. Chances to impress her were rarer still, because Connie did not make a habit of allowing herself to be impressed. But if you were not on form, she never missed a trick. It was said that she had never been known to forget a mistake—that anyone other than herself had made.

WPC Price had never known for certain whether Detective-Inspector Constance Kimble had seriously considered the possibility that Henry Gower might be innocent.

"There's a *prima facie* case on the file. On the evidence, the magistrates simply have to convict."

"Yes, ma'am."

They did not see much of Connie in the division—not that anyone complained on that score. In the St. Botolph's Fen End case she had had to be called down from Olympus; she'd have been slithering down the scree within two minutes of scanning the first Crime Complaint, anyway.

"Connie's right, you know," Sergeant Harrold said. "You've done a clear-cut job. Let the court sort it out."

Then the phone rang, and DC Warburton, being both the nearest and the most junior, picked it up. It could be frustrating, taking a call in the noisy CID room, but just for once there was something about his gravity that infected and silenced the others.

"Yes. Thank you. You can leave it to us."

It was the parents' solicitors, making a substantive complaint that Gower had been importuning young Davina. Sergeant Harrold took quiet command.

"Dicky, take Norman Purkis, go and bring Gower in. Clear case for arrest: contravening conditions of bail. Patsy—go and see what Davina Norris has to say. And I'll ring Connie. It would pay you to be on the scene before she is."

He was already reaching for switchboard to get him Central.

"And if anyone still fancies that Gower will get off, the odds are now worth having. Forties."

Warburton drove Patsy Price to St. Botolph's Fen End—a *Narrow Road with Passing Places*, once they had filtered out of the stream of heavy lorries on A17. They passed between fields without fences, separated by dykes three-quarters full of mud-brown, breeze-ruffled water. It was towards the end of March—signs of spring in swelling chestnut buds and patches of lesser celandine: but the nights were still sharply frosty. And it was not unknown for a peevish north-easter to blow in off the Wash from March to the end of June. They parted on the corner of School Close and St. Botolph's only other street. There would be nothing at the Norrises that a WPC could not handle on her own, and neither Warburton nor his companion expected trouble from as mild a character as Henry Gower.

Gower lived at the School House and had not yet moved out. He was suspended from duty, it went without saying, but as far as the Education Authority was concerned, it would be the verdict of the court that settled the issue. They could not evict a man who might not be found guilty. After a couple of days of enforced closure, a supply head teacher had been found to take charge of the small school. Gower was given to understand—and he agreed without argument—that he was not to set foot on the school premises until the affair had been determined. Nor was he to approach any of his former pupils.

His home was that of a man committed to his vocation. It was lined with books, especially encyclopædias and compendia of visual aids. Even children's art had found its way into his house. The sort of picture that one saw on the walls of infant classrooms had been considered worth preserving in the comfort of a home. The Gowers had two children of their own, who had been sent away to an aunt in Lincolnshire while St. Botolph's Fen End remained as traumatic for them as it was at the moment. A book on educational psychology lay on the arm of the chair where Henry Gower usually sat. How did he feel, still delving into the world from which he had been exiled with every prospect of no return? Or was he convinced that he was going to get off?

Mrs. Gower was sitting at a bureau, writing a letter on an ancient portable typewriter. She was a woman in the second half of her thirties, had obviously once been attractive in a no-nonsense way. But her first youth had slithered away from her and lack of sleep, loss of appetite and a clear vision of the likely future had etched lines of a deeper misery than she might admit to in words. Her husband was not at home.

"He's gone out on his bicycle. For a turn round the lanes. To try to clear his mind, he said. He's found it overfacing, hardly daring to show his face by daylight."

Warburton could well believe that. Gower was a thinking, sensitive man, a man with unusual ideas, a caring conscience and a turn of originality. Three months ago no one would have believed that he would be facing charges as a pervert. But educationally and in the social life of church and village he liked now and then, in his quiet way, to startle. It was for this reason that there were many who thought that there could be an element of truth behind the girls' allegations. Norfolk villages do not like to be startled.

"He didn't find it overfacing to show himself in broad daylight this afternoon," Warburton said. "It seems he scared Elsie Frost, then took Davina Norris for a walk."

"I know. I'd told him it was an idiotic thing to do. I knew what would happen if he did. He wouldn't take any notice. He said he was an honest man, and he wasn't afraid of the consequences of honest behavior."

"You mean he went out on purpose to speak to the girls?"

"He's been talking of doing it for days. He says he's not had a chance to speak to one of them alone since—since the day they say it happened. That's all he needed, he said, ten minutes alone with one of them. It was the way they stuck together that was making them perpetuate their lies." ·

"So he had to go and accost them in full view of the village? With half the mothers waiting at the school gates?"

"He said that was proof for all to see that he had no ill motives. There was a street full of witnesses that he had done nothing wrong."

Always, when talking to either of the Gowers, Warburton had had the same impression of translucent—and tragic—sincerity.

"All he wanted was to reason with one of them. To appeal to her decency to stop telling lies. I suppose the Norrises have complained? Or are the whole lot of them ganging up again?"

Warburton remained professionally tight-lipped on the point.

"I dare say I would too, if our positions were reversed," she said.

"Did your husband give you any idea how long he was likely to be?"

"No, but he can't possibly be long. He has no lights on his bike, and he's so law-abiding it isn't true."

Casa Mia was not one of the adapted cottages of the old village. It had been custom-built in the late 1950s—and there was nothing about its lines to call for the Spanish language. It had no windows at the front, except for narrow lights up the well of a staircase. It had a bulbous balcony almost along the whole width of its western elevation, and a protruding turret at its north-eastern corner. People had been heard to wonder how planning permission had ever been granted—but the house had never lacked occupiers prepared to pay outrageous asking prices. It had had three owners in its first fifteen years, and the Norrises claimed to have fallen in love with it at sight.

"I said they should never have let him out on bail."

That was Mrs. Cynthia Norris, talking while she was still showing WPC Price into the house. She was a woman of the right age to have had Davina not long after her twentieth birthday. She was plumpish, probably always had been, and it looked likely that before too long she would be carrying more fat than would suit her frame. She was wearing a shortened kimono displaying calves that were beginning to be flawed by varicosity. Had she just got out of a bath—though she must have been expecting an official caller at any moment? WPC Price wondered how many bottles of gin she killed in an average week.

"We don't keep possibly innocent people behind bolts and bars unless they're likely to abscond," Patsy Price said.

"What are you trying to say, Miss Price? That my daughter is a liar? You've given me the impression all along that that's what you think."

"That isn't for me to decide."

"If he had a shred of decency in him, he'd plead guilty and save these girls from having to go through that torment in public."

"Well—it doesn't look as if that's the way he is going to plead."

"Doesn't that business this afternoon prove that he shouldn't have been left at large?"

"That's what I've come to find out. What exactly did happen this afternoon?"

"He got on to her. He made her go for a walk with him."

"I'd like to hear her own account of it."

"She's out."

"Out?"

Davina wasn't exactly suffering from nervous prostration, then.

"She's round at Pauline Dean's. I suggested it. I thought it might take her out of herself. I expect they're listening to records."

Pauline Dean. Another of them. Three families relatively new to the village. You could drop the word "relatively" as far as the instincts of the natives were concerned. Norfolk people were not by nature discourteous to strangers—but it could take a quarter of a century for them to trust them. Three bright girls had arrived to enliven a little village school that had not very often had a look-in in the secondary selection charts. The Eleven Plus still operated here at this time and Davina, Pauline, Karen and Elsie would pass into the High School this year for a certainty—Elsie Frost was a clever but distinctly local girl, thrown together with the others because she was capable of the same work. Their parents had brought to Henry Gower's PTA the sort of life that had never been seen on a St. Botolph's Fen End committee before. They had attended evening classes taught by Gower so that they could help their children with the New Mathematics. They had raised funds, had bought the school a learners' swimming pool, had pressed for their children to be taught French, had inspired a summer term's outing to Whipsnade—much further afield than pre-Gower St. Botolph's would ever have dared to think of. That was before things had gone sour. When had things started to go sour? Had it been before these charges of indecent assault had been brought against their headmaster?

"It will be dark soon," Patsy Price said, as much to be provocative as in pursuit of facts. "You're not worried about Davina coming home alone?"

"The Deans will bring her home if she stays over the odds."

"Does that often happen?"

"We help each other out over things like that. It isn't our

daughters who ought to be under lock and key, Miss Price."

"I *shall* need to speak to her, you know. If she doesn't come soon, perhaps I could go round to the Deans' and fetch her."

"And have the entire village watching you—and concocting new theories?"

"Have they been concocting new theories?"

"I'm sure you know very well the sort of thing I am talking about, Miss Price."

"Can you give me a quick run-down of what happened this afternoon, Mrs. Norris?"

"He pestered her."

"About?"

"Do you need to be told?"

"In a word: yes, I do. My guesses aren't evidence."

"About withdrawing the charges. About what great friends they used to be. About saying it has all been a tissue of lies. About how things had got out of hand, about how they'd got more and more frightened, and then hadn't dared to change their story."

Mrs. Norris stopped, as if none of this was worth repeating.

"And that's all?"

"Isn't it enough? Wasn't it written into his bail that he was to have nothing to do with any of them?"

"Yes, it was—and that's being dealt with while we're talking."

"So I should hope."

"Did he touch her at all?"

"He put his hands on her shoulders."

The fool—

"And that's a technical assault," Mrs. Norris said.

"That will all be taken into account."

"Miss Price, I have to say this: I haven't liked your attitude since this business started, and I don't like it now. You've been on Gower's side since you first set foot in the village. And if you people hadn't taken our resident policeman away from us, it might never have happened."

"Decisions about posting village policemen are not taken by WPCs."

"I should hope not. It will all be taken into account, you say: another page of typing with a few carbon copies that you can send to each other for information. Can you not put yourself in the position of these girls?"

Yes: and a few people might try putting themselves in Henry Gower's shoes too, if only as a salutary exercise. But Patsy Price had to steer clear of saying anything of that nature. Cynthia Norris was already working herself up.

"Miss Price, I wish to reserve this discussion until I can deal direct with your Inspector Kimble."

"As you wish. But we are losing valuable time, and it is very necessary for me to speak to your daughter at once. In your presence, of course. So am I to go to the Deans' to fetch her, or will you go, or shall we both go, or will you ring the Deans?"

"Miss Price, I am not prepared to be ordered about like this."

It was at this stage that Cynthia Norris lost control. Admittedly these four families in St. Botolph's had been under tremendous strain. Except for the Frosts, they were not run-of-the-mill St. Botolph's people. Nigel Parbold was an accountant who as treasurer had pulled the PTA together. Jack Dean was a self-employed computer consultant, persuading small businesses that they needed the tailor-made programs that he could put together for them. Brian Norris lived under the colourable banner of *Company Director*, in some realm not spelled out to the general public, but whose perks were there for all to see—the maroon Mercedes, the frequent flights from Norwich airport. Even Bert Frost was an agricultural labourer who might more realistically have been called a technician. He knew as much about tractor-maintenance and fungicide sprays as he did about livestock.

But they were all—and more especially their wives—at the mercy of village speculation. They were all dreading the week in which their offspring would face Henry Gower's lawyer in the witness-box: his teachers' union had briefed counsel. It meant domestic upheaval, as well as intolerable suspense under the public eye. They all needed assurance that their children had suffered no lasting psychological harm. WPC Price tried to keep herself perpetually reminded of all this. In the Force they were always being exhorted to remember that it was humans they were dealing with. Even Connie pressed that party line—though she herself was not given to sparkling demonstrations of it, where her own rank and file were concerned.

Patsy Price was for ever struggling to identify with everyone she had to deal with: that was a short cut, the manuals assured her, to understanding motivation. But for all her study of the St. Botolph's Fen End elite set, she would never have predicted that Cynthia Norris would be the first to be seen to break. Cynthia Norris was tasteless, mindless, strident and unaccustomed to have to wait for anything she fancied in a magazine advertisement. Her husband appeared to derive his greatest satisfaction from showing the world that his Cynthia had today what they would want tomorrow.

"WPC Price, I take the strongest possible exception to your attitude. Ever since you first set foot in this village you have treated us as if we are the ones to be disbelieved."

Her face had reddened, and a shrillness had risen in her voice that she usually managed to keep filtered out of it.

"You have done nothing but insinuate that we are stirring up a mare's nest."

This was unfair and untrue. All that Patsy Price had ever done was to try not to take Henry Gower's guilt for granted. According to a standard textbook, eleven out of every twelve allegations of sexual offences were false, generated by spite, jealousy, revenge—or the need for attention and variety.

"I simply refuse to have any further dealings with you, Miss Price. Pick up that phone here and now and put me in touch with your Inspector Kimble. Are you going to do as I say?"

She shouted this as an absurd command, no longer

answerable to herself for the figure she was cutting. Patsy Price did move towards the phone—but it was not to contact Connie. She reached for the directory to look up the Deans' number.

"Don't you even know the number of your own office?" Mrs. Norris asked her.

Patsy did not get as far as dialling. There were the sounds of tyres on the pea-gravel of the drive. A car door slammed, and the Norrises' muffled chime-bars rang. Mrs. Norris was on her feet as if she did not know she had stood up, the prospect of another caller not diminishing her hysteria.

"Go and see who that is."

It was not hard to bite back the assertion that she was not a servant. Patsy had learned to let such irrelevancies flush over her like warm surf on a summer beach. She went to the door. Connie came straight in past her and clearly weighed up Cynthia Norris's condition in a split second—jumping no doubt immediately to every possible erroneous conclusion.

"You're here in the nick of time, Inspector. Miss Price was just phoning you. I have declined to have any further dealings with her."

Constance Kimble was in every way the antithesis of Patsy Price. Patsy was short, stocky without entirely losing shape, and though every item in her uniform was correct, she never looked as if she cared much for ceremonial parades. Connie was tall and poised, invariably looked as if she was dressed in line waiting to have a medal pinned on her.

"All I have said to Mrs. Norris, Inspector—"

"Wait outside, Price."

Patsy was saved from explosion by some indelible memory from her training days. She went and stood out in the hall, gazing without appreciation at a three-quarters-abstract print of Cader Idris. She was ready to hate almost any Norris possession.

She could hear only occasional words of what was being said in the lounge. Mrs. Norris, continuing shrill, talked at length at first. Connie came in more forcefully as things developed—until it was she who was doing all the talking. Then she came out.

"Come with me, Price. We'll go to the Deans' together."

After she had shut the car door, she said, "You will find, now and then, Price, people whom you cannot expect to influence. Never make that an excuse too soon, of course, but it will happen now and again."

That, for Connie, was a comparatively sympathetic remark.

The Deans lived in what had previously been two semis—a double-dweller, as the local term had it, now knocked together. They were not badly off, but the accent here was on technology rather than ostentation. Mozart and Mahler LP sleeves suggested that the stacked hi-fi system was more than a showpiece, and there were small trophies for badminton and squash. The two young members of the family were doing homework at the same table. Jack Dean was designing algorithms on a pad of squared paper and the overweight Pauline—black hair in a clipped fringe, and with no visible signs that she was under the weather psychologically—was making a fair copy of a map of local farmers' fields with felt-tipped pens.

"We were thinking we might find Davina Norris here."

"No. We haven't seen Davina for a day or two."

"She hasn't been here this evening?"

"No."

Dean looked at his daughter.

"When did you last see Davina?"

"After school. Going for a walk with Mr. Gower."

"She could be at one of the others' houses. Would you like me to ring round?"

"Please."

But the Parbolds had not seen anything of Davina Norris either. The Frosts were not on the phone.

In view of the sundry comings and going to the village, Hannah Maslin had fixed a clothes-peg to her vital inch of curtain.

• 3 •

THE LIGHT WAS all but gone. On the western horizon the afterglow was no more than a relic of sullen pink. Constance Kimble saw ahead to the large-scale search that might have to be mounted—the dogs, the men called in from any sector from which they could be spared, including their days off, a helicopter, if Air-Sea Rescue were not overloaded with their own work. They'd need frogmen: the fields were criss-crossed by a drainage system that went back to the seventeenth century. In the meanwhile they had to do what they could with what strength they could muster in the gathering darkness: an inexperienced WPC, DC Warburton and PC Purkis, his tenderfoot aide, a panda car when it could be released from a road accident on the King's Lynn northern bypass. Intercom was going to be bad.

It was the aide who found the bicycle—thrown down in the middle of a grass track that ran along a centuries-old sea-wall between two drainage dykes. Why should a man abandon his cycle in a spot like that? He must have cast it down pretty roughly: the end of one pedal had scored an inch or two of furrow in the soil and one brake-handle was slightly bent back. What would impel a man do a thing like that? Why dismount, and then continue on foot? There was no other evidence that Purkis could see as to what might have happened here. The only certain thing was that Gower had come this way—and had gone no further on wheels.

Constance Kimble did an almost frantically rapid inquiry from door to door. Had anyone seen Davina Norris this evening? The last door at which she knocked was Hannah Maslin's, where her reception was surly—and not just the localized misanthropy of someone who had it in for the fuzz. This was a thoroughgoing hatred of mankind, with a bonus for any woman who looked, spoke and treated people as Constance Kimble did.

The Inspector had no previous information about Hannah Maslin. Her fearsomely slatternly appearance took even a case-hardened senior policewoman aback. But she was quick to notice the clothes-peg on the curtain and the position of the old woman's chair close by it. Connie might not be the most popular officer among those answerable to her, but no one had ever accused her of not being on the ball.

"That's how you keep your eye on what goes on in St. Botolph's, is it?"

Hannah Maslin said nothing. She fixed Constance Kimble with a defiant eye.

"So perhaps you can tell me who's been on the move tonight."

"I don't know what you're getting at."

"What's happened tonight that doesn't usually happen in St. Botolph's? What's been worth watching?"

Mrs. Maslin wheezed. The Inspector could not make up her mind whether it was through stupidity or guile that she was determined not to cooperate. She believed it was characteristic of the Fen folk to practise guile for its own sake, irrespective of what they might have to gain or lose from it. It was printed into their genes centuries ago, when they were holding out behind their marshes against potential invaders of their empire.

"Who've you seen? Have you seen a little girl? Davina Norris? Do you know Davina Norris?"

"Of course I do. Everybody knows Davina Norris."

"When did you last see her?"

"Going down Mill Lane."

"This afternoon, you mean?"

"Tonight. More than an hour ago. You people don't know the half of what goes on," Hannah Maslin said.

The Inspector decided at least to try the effect of reasonable cajoling. Patsy Price might think it rare for her to produce an encouraging tone, but she could command a species of charm when she saw that a professional process required it.

"We don't claim to be magicians, you know. We're no stronger than the help people give us."

Hannah Maslin's only reaction was to look provocative. The Inspector knew the signals. They did not necessarily mean that the old woman was either a criminal or mentally defective. In her daily dealings she undoubtedly operated with a supreme cunning. Everyone she had to do with was a potential enemy. But her life had been so circumscribed, her expectations were so niggardly, her contacts with society so limited that she would have considered it a crime against herself to risk cooperating with a busybody stranger.

"I know what I know," she said.

Something raged inside Constance Kimble, but she suppressed it. There was no point in wasting time on Hannah Maslin here and now. If anything untowards had happened to Davina Norris, a couple of minutes gained now might still save her life.

"Do you or do you not know anything that you know you ought to tell me?"

"I know plenty."

"You saw Davina Norris go down Mill Lane for a second time today—this evening?"

"The schoolmaster too."

"What time was this?"

"Getting on for eight o'clock."

A shifting glint in Mrs. Maslin's eye. She knew very well what was relevant. She knew what could make trouble for people.

"He was out on his bike."

"I know that. But did you see him come back?"

"He was coming down the road the same time as the girl was turning into the lane."

"So he didn't go back to the School House?"

"He went down Mill Lane. After her."

"But did you see him come back?"

"They didn't come back this way."

Hannah Maslin was enjoying every subtle flavour of the mischief that was brewing. If she could throw anything into the stew, she would.

"You ought put the blame where the blame's due," Hannah Maslin said.

"What do you mean by that?"

"Don't you know?"

"I haven't time to play guessing games," Constance Kimble told her tartly. She hurried out of the house, only to find yet another hindrance awaiting her: Bert Frost, twentieth-century Hodge, expert on fungicides, insecticides and father of one of the other girls.

"Could I have a word, Inspector?"

"I haven't a second to spare."

"This is important."

"Make it quick, then. Come with me in my car. I'm not going far. We can talk on the way."

Frost was a youthful, sparingly-built man. He spoke with the Fenman's rhythm and intonation—which did not mean that he was inarticulate. He was what the twentieth-century agricultural labourer had become, a mixture of technologist and mechanic. But there was something indefinable about him that still proclaimed his origins in earth and furrow. The Inspector remembered his wife as a small, mousey woman, invariably worried. Elsie, their eleven-year-old, was the puniest, the most timorous, the only one underdeveloped of the quartet who had been involved in Gower's lapse. Frost took all aspects of his life with a desiccated seriousness: his home-making, his work, the upbringing and the prospects of his daughter.

The Inspector inserted her ignition key.

"Yes, Mr. Frost?"

"It's about—this business. I don't know how you're going to take this, Inspector."

"Try me."

"Elsie had a kind of breakdown tonight. She's telling us now that none of what they've been saying is true."

"They've been maintaining a solid front about it for six weeks," the Inspector said. "I put a lot of pressure on them myself during more than one session. They didn't waver."

She drove slowly to the Mill Lane turning, signalled as punctiliously as if she were driving in city traffic.

"I know," Frost said. "It's beyond belief—beyond my belief, anyway. I sometimes wonder if I live in the same world as other people. The world's changed a lot since I was eighteen."

The Inspector turned into Mill Lane, cruising slowly along it, scanning the road ahead and its flanks. There was the wreck of an old fen drainage pumping station some hundred yards in front of them, the boarding across its windows broken, its brickwork in bad need of pointing, the coping of its tall chimney chipped and irregular.

"When I think of the things they could tell you! Girls of eleven and twelve! And how they got everything right!"

The Inspector did not say anything. She was not as easily shocked as Frost was. Sex could obsess anyone, of any age. But the new possibilities gave food for more than one line of thought. She was not ready to believe anything until she had gone into it herself—not even the new line that Elsie Frost was taking.

"I mean, they could even say what Henry Gower's John Thomas was like," Frost said.

"Yes. They seemed well informed."

She braked at the entrance to the field track that led to the mill.

"I don't even know how to talk to my own daughter any more. I don't trust myself to handle this. But at the end of the day, you know. I blame—"

"Can we go into this later? And would you come with me, please? I could do with an extra pair of eyes."

The post-and-rail gate was chained and padlocked. She climbed it—with greater agility than Frost.

"What are we looking for?"

"Davina Norris. Or Henry Gower. Or both. Or anything else we find."

The pumping station—in reality an old engine-house—looked in silhouette a little like a Cornish tin mine. It was a landmark of not very frequent but fairly obvious resort—its interior as a public lavatory, its immediate surrounds as an *al fresco* courting-ground. There was detritus from both activities, some of it apparently recent. In a slight hollow behind the dilapidated building someone had dumped an old kitchen cooker, bald tyres and a discarded television set. It was also said to be haunted: there had once been a suicide there. Inspector Kimble had no patience with that kind of talk. She passed her torchlight over the immediate vicinity. Already the twilight had swallowed the skyline and nothing short of a line of men abreast could do justice to the adjacent fields. She pushed open the rotting door. It had been made fast over the years by a series of padlocks, the latest of which looked as if it had been wrenched out of its hasp months ago. There was nothing to be seen inside except fallen bricks and old rubbish.

"There's nothing we can hope to find here tonight," she said at last, leading the way back to her car. "You were saying something about who is to blame—"

"Doesn't that stand out a mile?"

"I'd rather hear you say outright what you have on your mind."

"Davina Norris. She's not normal, that child. She's not natural. My wife and I have known ever since we first set eyes on her that she was not the sort of friend we want for Elsie. I don't think the others care for her all that much, either."

"Girls like that often work on each other's imagination and nerves."

"But can there be any doubt about who's always in the lead? We've cudgelled our brains about what we could do about it. But what *can* you do, in a place as small as this, all going to the same school? You can't stop kids from playing with each other. You can't say, 'Don't have anything to do with So-and-So.' "

They were driving past smallholdings and the Inspector was looking out keenly to see whether any man was still out squeezing a last few minutes on his rows—someone who might have seen a man or child pass.

"She has had Elsie petrified," Frost said. "And the other two the same. I don't think we've unearthed the half of it yet. But we mean to get to the bottom of it."

"It's as unsavoury a business as anything I've ever handled, Mr. Frost—"

Why was she saying that? It was always sound policy not to reveal one's state of mind to a witness while he was still volunteering information.

"Let's just hope that the consequences haven't already gone too far."

She was beginning to fear very vividly that they might have done.

"You see, I don't even know how to take what she's telling us tonight. She might just be saying it because she's scared of Gower. He was crossing the road to talk to her this afternoon. She came home screaming and upset."

Norman Purkis had not been an aide to CID for more than a week. Up to now it had amounted to no more than accompanying Dicky Warburton on his rounds, taking down statements, guarding bolt-holes; but it was a heaven-sent break from General Duties, as well as perhaps being the first rung towards the plainclothes list himself. It was only when he found himself alone for the first time that he began to realize what it was like to be faced with a decision on a seemingly trivial matter that could go catasrophically wrong in a second. What to do now he' had found the bicycle? Go back the way he had come and report it—if he could find anyone to report it to? Or leave it unattended,

open to interference, while he went on ahead to look for its
rider?

He opted for the latter, walked on another thirty yards,
stopping frequently to stare into the dusk round the points of
the compass. He saw nothing that told him anything about
Henry Gower. A detective was supposed to be able to make
a landscape talk to him, to see any minor interference with
the normal layout of things from which he could retrace an
unaccustomed event. Within a few more minutes it would
be impossible to see a thing. He could discover nothing
informative: only the winter-sown wheat, looking sturdy
enough, and a chilly-looking ripple across the waters of the
dykes.

He went on another hundred yards, saw the headlamps of
a car along the far border of a strawberry-field, did not
realize that that was Connie Kimble and Frost on their slow
cruise. A reverse ripple struck diagonally across the water
as a current of air changed course: a draught blowing like a
thin blast through a brick culvert. He shone the disc of his
lamp into the darkness of the arch, and saw that the conduit
was choked with rubbish, a sackful of it, as if someone had
dumped a bag of old cement. And then there was a stirring
of adrenalin in his veins as he recognized that this was a
body—head-first and face-downwards in the narrow tunnel.
If the light had been good enough to make out colours, he
would have seen that the apparent milkiness hanging static
for inches round the edges of the corpse was red blood. He
got down on his hands and knees to drag the body out by its
feet, in case there remained any hope of resurrection. But
pulse and breathing had stopped. If stabbing and slashing
had not done their work, drowning had. Purkis had never
met Henry Gower, but he guessed who it was, and did not
doubt that he had come to Henry Gower's last resting-place.
But the rule-book said try, and Purkis tried. He had never
done mouth-to-mouth before, except on a trainer's dummy.
The experience was to make him want to vomit for a long
time.

* * *

The ambition and purpose of Mill Lane is to join Half Moon
Lane, which as its name suggests, swings round in an arc to
connect one extremity of St. Botolph's Fen End to the other.
It was Half Moon Lane that DC Warburton was now
walking with every sense tautened, looking in at every
orchard gate for anybody lurking. And then he came to the
end of the apple-trees and was skirting a field of strawber-
ries. Norman Purkis was walking parallel to one of its
longer sides, and Connie Kimble driving along the other,
straining her eyes into the now almost final gloom.

   Then he heard something plunge into a watercourse only
a pace or two behind him, far too heavy for a water-vole.
He thought perhaps it was a coypu, at present a pest in these
parts. But a young detective-constable with his fame to
establish does not assume that on a night when he is hoping
to make a vital discovery, the first weird phenomenon will
be common vermin. He turned and took a step in the
direction of the disturbance. Something fell foul of the
bulrushes which clogged a corner of the ditch. He took a
pugnacious step towards the movement. Whatever it was
moved again—and then there was a splash and something
fell clumsily into the water with a strikingly human cry of
appeal. He plunged in water up to his waist, hauled a
struggling child out on to the bank. It was Davina Norris.

• 4 •

THE CONVERSATION IN the CID Room, shallow water at slack tide-time, clung predictably to the obvious. If the kids had invented the stories they had told about Henry Gower, then their precocity must be phenomenal. Only Detective-Sergeant Harrold, who had no more than another year to go, offered his own brand of scepticism.

"So what? The first thing Connie did when she moved in on the case was to get them to give her a description of Gower's cock. Was he circumcised? How long was it? Its approximate girth? Colour scheme? Warts, wens and battle-scars. Specifications of his scrotum. Did it have a seam like a cricket ball? Which one hung lower than the other? Gower confidently submitted to a medical, but it did rather look as if they had been talking about the right set of tackle. So what does that signify? I've got one, you've got one, Connie and Patsy haven't—but I dare say they've seen line drawings, even if they haven't actually handled the real thing in their own right. There's nothing about a penis, in the factual sense, that a girl of twelve can't know. I don't suppose they talk about much else, those that have started taking an interest."

"Which of them hasn't? But they did all agree, Sarge."

"All except the Frost kid, who said she didn't look properly, because it made her feel sick. I'd have been more impressed if they hadn't agreed quite so neatly with each other. Different kids ought to have come up with slightly different impressions—but these young angels didn't. They all saw the same plonker and they painted the same word-picture of it."

"Collusion, then?"

"Well, since we're now asked to believe that they didn't see it, it must have been either that or extra-sensory perception. And even pukka experiments in that sphere come up with variations. Yet not these four innocents. They all displayed the same photographic memory of Gower's tool. I reckon one or the other of them has caught sight of it at some time or other. They have been on School Camps with him, and they probably spent half their time lying about in hedge-bottoms waiting for him to unbutton his flies."

If Davina Norris had been an adult, rather than a cossetted adolescent, she could well have been held for custodial investigation. She might even have been charged before the night was out. The child was unable to offer any articulate description of what she had witnessed—indeed it was not clear whether she had witnessed anything at all. She could give no consistent account of how she came to be where she was found—or where else she had been, or why. She had no convincing explanation of how she came to be out of doors in the first place, except that it was apparently not at all unusual, when late evening prowling caught her fancy, for her to come quietly down the stairs and let herself out of the kitchen door while her mother was watching television. Where did she go on such expeditions? She liked solitude; she said she *needed* solitude. She liked darkness. She often felt claustrophobic indoors: she used that word.

She was a precocious child—and her advanced intelligence did nothing to render her attractive. She said that she could *think* better in the open air. She projected an image of herself in the mould of an early nineteenth-century poet confiding his *mal de siècle* to the elements.

Had she come out tonight with the intention of meeting anyone? She strenuously denied that: human society was something she wanted to escape from, not consort with.

There were moments when she seemed to be talking like a little soured old lady. When Dicky Warburton hauled her from the dyke she was shaken. They got her back to where they could try to talk to her rationally and Connie tried to wheedle what essentials she could from her, while not losing sight of the imprudence of putting pressure on a child in shock. They had to get her to medical attention without delay: minutes could be vital. Davina was confused—but she was also so obviously an intuitive actress that it was tempting to suspect her of simulating her confusion, or at least of exaggerating it. She seemed to know that Henry Gower had been killed—and yet there were moments when she seemed to forget that.

Even if she had had the strength to have stabbed him, she could not conceivably have raised his corpse and pitched it face downwards into the culvert where Purkis had found it. She could not have thrust and twisted the dagger in his gut the way it had been thrust and twisted. Could she, would she, have slashed at his genital organs in the way that Gower had been slashed? Was Connie in danger of ruling this out only because she was a juvenile? No; because if there had been any scuffling at all between Henry Gower and a child, the child was bound to have been hurt—and as far as Connie could see, Davina Norris had not been hurt: no bruising from fingertips gripping her upper arms. Her calves and ankles were scratched, but that was accountable for by brambles, and one deeper gash by barbed wire.

Connie was taking a risk every second that she kept Davina from the medics. They took over with soap, water and sedatives and Davina Norris was hospitalized with rule-of-the-book caution. A WPC was deputed to stay as close to her as the hospital would permit—which was not close. She was to learn nothing. Davina was lost to the investigators until tomorrow morning at least—with the hint that access was not promised even then.

Connie sent Patsy Price round the houses of the other three children, to ascertain that they were home and, if the parents knew, whether they had been at home all the

evening. She also briefed her to find out anything the
parents could tell her about Davina Norris's habits of
circumambulating after dark. She was to bring the subject
up without creating more emotional disturbance than she
could help.

She went first to the Deans'. Jack Dean's domestic
lifestyle seemed to operate along the systems lines of his
vocation. He and his wife nurtured their only child with
rational faith in contemporary psychology. (Helen Dean had
been a teacher, and had followed a couple of Open
University courses on child development.)

No: they were absolutely certain that Pauline had not left
the house in the evening without their authority and knowledge of where she was going. It was inconceivable, in the
light of the bonds that existed between them and their child,
that such a thing could happen. Deceit was a word that had
no place in the ethos of this family.

So had any whisper ever come to their ears via Pauline
that it was not unheard-of for Davina Norris to go wandering forth, escaping from claustrophobia into darkness?
Well—not in so many words. Not in so many words? What
exactly did they mean by that? Oh, nothing: loose talk.
Certainly Pauline had never hinted at anything of the sort
about her friend. Did it come as a surprise to them, then,
that Davina had been out and about tonight? Helen and Jack
Dean exchanged glances that WPC Price did not miss. She
was sure they were on the verge of saying that nothing that
Davina Norris ever did would surprise them—but that was
the sort of thing that the Deans were too disciplined to say.
Nothing made sense to them that could not be programmed.

"I wonder what you're going to say when I tell you that
one of the girls is now claiming that nothing in their
allegations against Mr. Gower was true?"

"I'll say at once that I know which of the three that would
be. It would be Elsie Frost—chickening out because she's
afraid to give evidence. Didn't she scream hysterically at
the sight of Gower this afternoon?"

"But just suppose it is the truth she's telling now?"

"It won't be."

"What makes you so sure?"

"Pauline would never have told us untruths about something of this magnitude. Not that I'm saying she'd tell us lies about anything. Nor am I saying she's never been naughty in her time—in the usual trivial ways. She's just a perfectly normal child."

"Well, tell her what's being said now—and that one of us will be round to talk to her about it in the morning."

Patsy Price went off to see two other pairs of disturbed parents.

• 5 •

"WE DON'T KNOW each other, Sergeant Parrott."

"No, sir. Though of course I've heard of your—reputation."

Coy—tongue in cheek. Kenworthy did not rise to it, drove up to the limit against the ground-swell of early morning traffic, lost behind a screen of concentration.

Things had moved fast. Beetfields, bicycles and cesspits—Norfolk might still have an earthy image—but somebody out there believed in getting things moving.

Immediately murder was apparent, a message was got to their Detective Chief Superintendent Arnold Blane via Norwich. That was standing orders, no matter where Blane was or what he was doing. The message reached him about eight o'clock, in the dining-room of a clifftop golf-club south of Cromer. One of the Deputy Chiefs happened to be dining in the same room.

"You'll make this one our own, Arnold?"

"I can keep a general eye on it, but it wouldn't be safe for me to take the case. Too much security on my plate. State visit to Sandringham and Special Branch will be asking for something fresh every five minutes."

"So who?"

"It'll have to be Tom Wilson. There's only one thing—"

The Deputy Chief raised inquiring eyebrows.

"There'll be a heavy woman's angle."

"Connie?"

"She'll be answerable to Tom, of course."

"Better get the Londoners in."

That decision was made by ten past the hour and confirmed by the Chief himself within the next five minutes.

Arnold Blane occupied an even cloudier reach of Olympus than Constance Kimble. He frequently claimed that he saw his role not as commander, but as coordinator and enabler, thanks to which outlook he was always unquestionably in command. Like a general directing an army corps, he had access to reserves that he could move around into hard-pressed positions—heavy artillery that could bring fire to bear on fronts when they looked like cracking. It was also rumoured that he could keep officers like Connie on the rails when they showed signs of uptightness. He seldom played much part in the hand-to-hand fighting himself—unless a subordinate asked him to, which did sometimes happen. The basic team at Kenworthy's disposal had to include Connie, since she had her finger on the pulse of the case already. At her best, Connie could be good—and when Blane was about, she was at her best. Chief Inspector Tom Wilson, from the Broadlands, would establish and direct the operational HQ that Kenworthy would need. He had the edge of rank over Connie, so was officially rated officer in charge on the spot—a subtlety to be kept in reserve for emergencies—and an indication of Blane's shrewdness as a tactician.

Patsy Price was also going to be kept in St. Botolph's, although Blane knew that there had been bad blood between her and Connie during the first phase of the case. Detective-Constable Dicky Warburton and PC Norman Purkis, still on loan from uniform branch, were to be on hand for dogsbodying. They already knew the area, and some of the personalities. Detective-Sergeant Harrold was not going to be involved. He was left among the depleted body dealing with any residual Fenland wickedness—but this would not prevent him from taking a keen sardonic interest in what was going on—or from giving impartial pontifical advice whether it was appreciated or not.

Norfolk's request was at the Yard by a quarter to ten. Within five minutes it was referred to the Commander who had to make the executive decisions.

"Kenworthy, leave notes for Mike Quigley—*all* your notes about Operation Matchbox. You're going out among the beet-bashers. I expect you're still in the habit of keeping a bag packed? I'll send you a teleprint of all that's known so far, as soon as I can get one together. I'll have a rider stick it through your letter-box within the next three hours. I haven't found a sergeant for you yet. I'm giving that a lot of thought. I'll be in touch."

The telex arrived a little after midnight. Shortly after that, the phone rang. Elspeth took it: a woman's voice. Her eyes lit up with a mischievous light.

"Your latest helpmeet, Simon—Sergeant Parrott."

Kenworthy did not know her. She sounded like someone in the third-year sixth at one of the more sheltered young ladies' seminaries.

"Early start, Sergeant Parrott," Kenworthy said. "Very early start indeed. Where do you live?"

"Winchmore Hill."

"I'll pick you up. Five-fifteen."

Kenworthy spent half an hour with the teleprint, then went to bed, setting his alarm for four o'clock.

"No—as you say, Sergeant Parrott, we don't know each other—except for such of my reputation as has penetrated into your corner of the panhandle. I won't embarrass you by craving detail about that."

They had driven twenty-five miles since she had made the remark. It was almost ten minutes since either of them had spoken. Polly Parrott, twenty-seven, tall, slender, elegant and nicely-spoken to the point of excruciation, looked as if she could easily make herself look sixteen if a case demanded it.

"What have they taken you off to come and keep me on the feminist rails, Sergeant?"

"Operation Coldframe, sir: provincial girls, missing, believed somewhere in London."

"So you're into the adolescent scene?"

"Pre-adolescent, mostly."

"On shoulder-rubbing terms with quite a deal of nastiness?"

"One gets used to it."

"Pity."

"Sorry?"

"I said, that's a pity. Never cease to be shocked, Sergeant Parrott. Try not to become inured. The moment we cease to be disgusted at the stuff we spend our time on, we lose nine-tenths of our fire. I've got a feeling we're going to need to smoulder a bit in Norfolk."

A few minutes later he pulled into a lay-by and asked her to take the wheel. She wondered whether he had waited to get clear of outer London before trusting himself to her driving.

"I have homework to do."

By the light of a pencil torch he did his best to read again the hastily cobbled pre-case history that the Commander had sent him. Dawn seemed reluctant to put an end to night. The first grey remained for a long time a low-key and uninformative grey. They put behind them the last of the dual carriageways, took to secondary roads that meandered round the edges of farm fields without wreaking too much havoc with ancient boundaries. They passed through the centre of an unlit town. Kenworthy halted them again, so that they could agree in advance about the next spell of map-reading. It was in a most unlikely neighbourhood—a grid of single-track lanes, culverts and hump-backed bridges that they found themselves slowing down in the rear of a short convoy, two of the cars flashing blue roof-lights: somebody else was making an early start.

They pulled up at the edge of a dyke, got out of their cars and converged on a gateway into a field. Self-introductions were brief, unsatisfying, confusing. Kenworthy had confounded his Norfolk colleagues by arriving as early as this.

They probably hadn't expected him before mid-morning, maybe not until lunch-time. They would not have a head-quarters set up yet, probably hadn't even got their paper-work into a state they'd consider fit to hand over.

Constance Kimble had brought a small team, including a uniform sergeant from King's Lynn, to look at the ground that it had been impossible for her to examine properly last night. They climbed the grassy sea-wall. It was a bleak prospect, crisp rime on grass and cabbages, an unrelenting wind blowing in from the estuary, a dispiriting flatness in every direction. The place where Norman Purkis had found Henry Gower's bicycle looked as if it could not possibly be made to yield information.

About fifty yards away, they found the spot where it looked as if Gower had actually been killed. It was in the middle of the field, well away from the track along which he had been cycling. There was ample confirmation that a struggle had taken place. The topsoil had been soggy when it happened and was still frost-hardened, so that it showed where feet had trampled—though the surface had not preserved a useful sole-print. At one point both bodies must have rolled on the ground, but the soil and grass gave away nothing more than that. It was obvious that Gower's assailant had been someone capable of putting up a fight with a vigorous forty-two-year-old: it could not possibly have been Davina Norris.

Gower had been dragged some fifty yards to the culvert. Daylight made it possible to detect the original spillage of blood in the rough pasture and there were smears along the route that he had been dragged. The place where Dicky Warburton had found Davina Norris behind the bulrushes was nearer to the death-spot than it was to the culvert.

"Shall we continue, Mr. Kenworthy?"

"Just carry on as if I weren't here."

Constance Kimble led on to the culvert. It was possible to see that the bed of the watercourse had been disturbed. Knowing that Purkis had dutifully gone through the motions of trying to resuscitate Gower, one could see where the body had lain and the aide had knelt. This was purely negative information, and otherwise there was nothing. Kenworthy guessed that Inspector Kimble was willing the surroundings to make known their secrets. But there was nothing but the unrelieved monotony of dormant fields, no significant growth yet awakened by the spring.

"I've brought Sergeant Dunne with me, Mr. Kenworthy. Part of his duties takes him round school bicycle sheds, inspecting pupils' machines. There are questions I'd like you to try to answer about Henry Gower's bike, Sergeant Dunne. Why were one spoke broken, and two spokes bent on the rear wheel? Why was there soil under the bottom edge of the front mudguard? Which way would a rider fall if his cycle was attacked from various angles? Can you work out the angle of his fall from the damage to the spokes? It seems obvious now why Gower stopped in his tracks. Someone stopped him in them. Do you think that while still in motion, his cycle was kicked from behind, from the left-hand side? It fell to its left. Look—there are scars in the topsoil to bear this out."

Kenworthy wrote her off as a tense woman. She was thinking aloud, the words tumbling out of her, herself answering the questions that she was hurling at Sergeant Dunne.

"There's a more fundamental question than that, Inspector," Kenworthy said. "Why was Gower riding along this track in the first place? It only leads between dykes and fields. What conceivable reason could he have for wanting to come this way? Especially as it must have been getting pretty dark."

"And we know he had no lights," Connie said.

"If, as you've just suggested, he was attacked from behind, would he not already have passed his attacker when that happened? If he had had any idea that he was about to be assaulted, would he not have dismounted?"

Had someone been lying in ambush? Constance Kimble went back to scramble down the bank beside the spot where Gower had been knocked off his cycle. She found no traces that anyone had lain in wait there: no cigarette-ends, no derangement of vegetation. A ripple enlivened the still life of the dyke. A clump of reeds leaned and rustled. If reeds had eyes, they would have seen what had happened. But reeds, ripples and waterweed were mute.

"Don't you think it was the sight of Davina Norris that made Henry Gower take to the fields?" Kenworthy asked. "It's known that she came out towards this way, isn't it? But what for? And what had been her relationship with whoever had killed Gower? There are a lot of imponderables, Inspector."

It was all very well trying to impress his country cousins with what he already knew. It did not form a continuous narrative, and he knew he could not keep it up for long. They were getting nowhere, and the rest of them must have been feeling as cold as he was. Kenworthy thought he heard Sergeant Parrott's teeth chattering.

"I suggest you get a team as soon as you can over every inch of these surroundings, Inspector Kimble. And for the time being, how about getting indoors, out of this frightful blast, so that you can fill me in on the details I know nothing about yet?"

"Chief Inspector Wilson is setting up a Report Centre for you in the Village Hall. But I don't know whether he'll have had time yet to do much more than find the caretaker and the key."

"At least, I live in the hope that the place has four windproof walls and some form of rudimentary heating. And incidentally, I'd be prepared to pay the going rate to any householder in St. Botolph's who would cook me an Englishman's breakfast."

Organizing this appealed immediately to Connie—he guessed because it would get him out of her hair for half an hour, give her a chance to alert CI Wilson and ginger up her own followers. It took her only a few minutes to find a cottager, the widowed Mrs. Race, who produced him a man-sized fry-up to which he applied himself while Sergeant Parrott played delicately with Rice Crispies.

"A terrible thing to have happened, sir. One terrible thing after another."

"Yes. And I suppose, in a village like this, you all know each other so well—"

"Well, sir, yes, sir—and no, sir. There are two kinds of people in St. Botolph's Fen End these days."

"I suppose so."

Constance Kimble came back in three-quarters of an hour's time, as if she had timed it to the minute. On the dyke-bank she had risked facing her public in an anorak and Wellingtons, but she was ready for parade again now—or at least for a modelling session based on what a potential woman Chief Constable should wear on her way up: a grey suit, uncrumpled from riding in small cars, a discreet but *de rigueur* cameo brooch.

"You now have a desk, sir—or, at least, a trestle table. We'll get a proper desk up from HQ later in the morning. Wood's burning in the stove. We've been promised that the telephone will be working in an hour. There's a modest log of papers for you to look over—"

"I expect I shall want to spend most of the morning talking to people. The Norrises are an obvious priority."

"Norris himself is away: Java, making up his mind about cinchona futures. His wife I'm afraid you're going to find a little elusive. She's coming and going to and from the hospital—*not* with enthusiasm, but making the most of the opportunities not to be where we'd like her to be. She has a natural skill in the art of not being helpful. Still—it's wrong of me to prejudice you."

"Not at all, Inspector. You are a highly trained observer. Trained observation is a totally different animal from prejudice."

She paused before putting her next question.

"Will you want me with you, Mr. Kenworthy, when you call on Mrs. Norris?"

Kenworthy paused too.

"I think not, Inspector. She knows you. I shall be an enigma to her. That could be useful."

"As you wish, sir."

A woman, he told himself, who could be very ready to take professional offence over pettinesses, but who was making a conscious effort to restrain herself from doing anything of that nature at this juncture.

"I may as well tell you, Inspector: as you probably know, I was sent a hasty abstract, very incomplete, as it was bound to be. I already have certain pictures in my mind. I know a little about the Norrises. I know that the Frosts are the odd people out in the quartet. I know that the micro-chip has entered into the souls of the Deans. I seem to have picked up nothing at all about the other family—the Parbolds."

"Yesterday evening was little short of frenzied, Mr. Kenworthy. When London asked for an interim telex, we had to draw the line somewhere. It was not until very late that my WPC Price was able to go and see the Parbolds."

"Perhaps I can have a word with WPC Price shortly, then."

"Her report is on your desk."

"I would like her to take me through it herself. There are certain to be things I shall want to ask her."

"As you wish."

• 6 •

PATSY PRICE LOOKED as Kenworthy remembered his own daughter looking, in her uncertain self-assessment period between college and her first job. She was small-framed, not particularly bothered what to do about her potential good looks. And she retained too much of her youth—in complexion, enthusiasm and vigour—to look ready yet for adulthood. Patsy Price was nervous into the bargain. She couldn't have sat much nearer the edge of her chair if Kenworthy had been HM Inspector of Constabulary. But he did nothing specific to put her at her ease. He wanted to watch her as she was. Her nerves were something she had to sort out for herself. If she took too long about it, he hadn't much hope for her as a career policewoman.

"You can tell me something about the Parbolds, I think."

"I was round there last night, sir."

"Tell me about them."

"Nigel Parbold has been out of work for the better part of a year. He calls himself an accountant, but he's not one, really. I mean, I'm not making him out to be a liar, but he isn't a *Chartered* accountant, or anything like that. He's taken some exams, though, and used to work in the office of a firm that's gone bankrupt on one of the King's Lynn industrial estates. You can tell he works with figures: his everyday life seems a bit like book-keeping. He doesn't think life has any problems that can't be solved by common sense and arithmetic. I've heard that from his own lips several times. It's funny: there are two families close to this case who live according to rules. They're very different, though. The Deans are all science and technology, call themselves agnostics. The Parbolds are chapel-people. They over-simplify everything. Mrs. Parbold—Jane—is a nonentity. She seems negative in everything she does. Even last night, in all the kerfuffle, there was hardly a cheep out of her."

There was certainly no lack of confidence in WPC Price, now that the key-log in the speech-dam had shifted. Kenworthy began to revise his opinion.

"You, of course, have talked to them more than once?"

"Yes—several times at the beginning of this Henry Gower business. They both seem to like dullness for its own sake—as if it were a sort of safety-net. Am I straying too far from the point, sir?"

"Just tell it your own way, Miss Price. And the word *sir* is music to my ears just twice a day: the first and the last time you see me."

"Thank you, sir—Mr. Kenworthy—I had to break the news to them, what had happened to Mr. Gower, and they were shocked to hear it. But it seemed to shock them even more when I told them that Davina Norris had been out on her own about the lanes last night. Nigel Parbold assured me that their Karen had not been out alone on this or any other evening. He insisted on taking me upstairs to see that she really was in her bed. And he was very cross because she had fallen asleep between her striped nylon sheets with a cassette player still switched on on her bedside table. He pulled the covers up about her shoulders so roughly that I thought he was trying to wake her and give her a good ticking off. She flung herself on to her other side and said something in her sleep—some word that I did not catch properly: it sounded like *Bisto*."

" 'It's that confounded puppet play,' Parbold said. 'It's wrought havoc with their nerves.' "

"What puppet play's that?" Kenworthy asked.

"Oh, something that Henry Gower wrote. He's always writing and producing plays for the school. Some of the parents think they do too much of it—there was something special in the first half of this term."

WPC Price described Karen Parbold's room. Pop music clearly played a big part in the child's life: a poster of Elton John, an autographed portrait of some group that she had seen on Yarmouth pier last summer—together with relics of outlived phases—a Beatrix Potter frieze and another of Awdry's tank-engines. And hanging on the wall was a hand-made marionette, a very creditable piece of handicraft—it was obvious that the finishing touches to both figure and clothing must have been contributed by adult hands. The character was a man in a black suit, with long chin and nose and a sardonic twist to his upper lip.

" 'We trust her to switch the light out without fail at eight o'clock,' Parbold said. 'She goes about looking tired all day—and is it to be wondered at?'

"He could not bear it for a stranger to see his house-rules being broken, even over such a trivial matter as this. I don't know: he seemed to be taking that more to heart than he was the news about Henry Gower. I asked him if he normally came up to look at her during the course of the evening?

" 'Invariably,' he said, but not very emphatically. You know how it is, when people are not telling the truth: they don't think it seems as bad, if they don't say it too loudly."

When they were downstairs again, Price had asked the question she had been repeating all the evening. Did Davina Norris's wanderings at night come as a surprise to them?

"Nothing would surprise us about Davina Norris."

"I asked why he said it in that tone.

" 'Because it's true,' he said. 'She's not normal. She's over-imaginative. Her mother's been heard to let slip the word *genius*—which didn't go down too well with some of the other parents who heard it, I can tell you. So is every other child in St. Botolph's Fen End a moron? Oh, she's an extraordinary child, there's no doubt about that. But less than a lovable one, in some people's estimation.' "

Parbold's wife had contributed nothing to the conversation, but she began to look anxious at the turn it was taking, and especially at her husband's anger, which did not subside. Indeed, he seemed to be consciously fuelling it.

" 'There have been times,' Parbold said, 'when, to tell you the truth, we haven't known what we ought to do about Davina Norris. But you can't make and unmake your children's friendships for them, can you? All you can do is to offer reasoned advice—but how can you expect a child of this age to know what you're really trying to tell her?'

" 'What sort of advice, Mr. Parbold—and on what particular occasions?'

" 'Not to let herself get carried away by others. Always to stick to what she knew was right. Not to be afraid to talk to her mother and myself about anything she was unhappy about.'

"I said that that made it sound as if he'd had reason to be apprehensive. What did he think she might have been unhappy about? And when? He said there had been this business with Gower.

" 'I mean, apart from that,' I asked him. 'Have you been apprehensive about anything else?'

" 'You know these girls have always had a great measure of freedom? We've always believed in giving them a pretty free rein, here in the country—as long as they stuck together, and promised not to go wandering off the beaten track. Not to trespass, for example. To keep off the land of those farmers who don't care for uninvited youngsters.'

"It was the first mention I'd heard of trespassing. I asked if there had been any history of it? Of hostile farmers?

" 'Not exactly. Karen has never actually trespassed—not to do any damage, not to make a nuisance of herself.'

" 'And she would tell us about it, if she had,' Mrs. Parbold said, unusually anxious to speak. 'She has always been absolutely open with us. That's something we have always been able to count on. She has never been an ounce of worry to us since the day she was born—not until this other horrible business.' "

"That horrible business is going to leave its mark for a very long time," Kenworthy said.

"'I'm afraid so,' I said. And now I had to tell them about Elsie Frost's bombshell. I don't think the Parbolds grasped the full implications immediately—and I wanted to get back to this word *trespass*. I didn't think I'd got all there was to be got out of it. It had meant far more to the Parbolds than I could see good reason for. So I came back to it. I asked him if there was anywhere in particular where he had forbidden Karen to go.

"'We mustn't go setting you on false trails, Officer. It isn't a nice place—but that's mostly due to foolish village talk. It's just that we're naturally concerned for our daughter's physical safety. You'll have seen that derelict old engine-house down Mill Lane? Obviously, it has always fascinated them.'

"'So you made it a no-go area?'

"'The place is structurally unsafe. It's dirty—a health hazard. It's a case of an absentee landlord, and the place isn't properly cared for. There are things thrown away there that you wouldn't want young girls to come across. We've tried to get the Parish Council to do something about it, but they always fall back on vague talk that it's of historical interest. The old beam engine was sent to a rural science museum years ago, but there's always been talk of putting up the cash to get it back and put it in working order. Of course, nothing ever happens.'

"'And the girls have been going there?'

"'We found out about it when they were practising their parts for the puppet play. They'd started using the old pumping-station as a headquarters. It was that odd character John Thurlow who told us about it. Or, at least, he spoke to Jane about it.'

"His wife was pale. She looked as if she felt she had to apologize for having had anything to do with John Thurlow. You'll see him about in the village, sooner rather than later. Everybody calls him *Sheriff*, because he goes about dressed like somebody out of the Wild West—nine-gallon hat, gunbelt, bandana. Oh, he's harmless enough—working out some fantasy—prolonged immaturity of some kind or other.

Yet in conversation you could mistake him for normal. You're expecting a Texas drawl, and all you get is a Norfolk accent. But he's a born interferer—in all sorts of things. He's always trying to stick his nose in—not that anybody takes much notice of him. But it seems he did come up to Mrs. Parbold in the street, and told her she ought to know that the children had been playing in the engine-house.

" 'I really don't know,' Mrs. Parbold said, 'why they should want to hang about in that filthy old place when every one of them has a warm, comfortable bedroom she can invite her friends to. Of course, we put a stop to it. If you ask me, that puppet play has a lot to answer for.'

"I asked her in what sense? Her husband seemed to think she had done enough talking for one evening, and answered before she could speak again.

" 'They became so intense about it. I'm not one of those who gets hot under the collar about modern educational methods. I used to admire Henry Gower for his ingenuity. No one could have supported him more strongly at PTA meetings than I did, until—' "

Until H-hour for St. Botolph's Fen End, a few weeks ago, when Gower had embarked on his next project after the puppets: a new programme of instruction on the human reproductive system, tailor-made for enlightened eleven-year-olds. One afternoon, at the end of school, four of his brightest had come to him, not without some touch of modest shyness, to ask for even further enlightenment: there were certain material details about reproductive procedures that were puzzling them. Henry Gower was alleged to have overdone the material detail. He had remained behind with the group when the rest of the pupils had gone home and had showed them things about himself and themselves from which little girls of that age are normally protected by the invocation of a sort of need-to-know rule. He had made them touch him and he had touched them. The object-lesson had included, they claimed, a demonstration of the mechanics of producing a male erection. It had fallen to Patsy Price to make the first prudently sceptical inquiries. Then Connie

Kimble had descended from the haunts of the gods to show her how to get to the heart of such matters.

"This puppet play?" Kenworthy asked.

"Oh, I suppose, basically, there was no harm in it. I didn't see the show, of course, but I've read the script. It was a modern version of the Faust theme, but comic, not philosophical, with apologies to Goethe and Marlowe. There were a lot of effects—explosions off-stage, and that sort of thing. And the key character was cast as a woman. In a way it was a bit of a skit against feminist extremists. That's why Gower called the play *Fausta*. Mephistopheles was a figure of farce—My God! That's what that child said in her sleep: *Mephisto*—not *Bisto*—"

WPC Price rolled her eyes towards the ceiling at the stupidity of her delayed reaction.

"That's who the puppet on Karen's bedroom wall was—Mephisto. And in the play, every time Mephisto thought he'd caught Fausta out, she did something devious to upset his plans. He was a comic devil, a devil always doomed to fail. I thought it was quite clever. But I'm not sure that it was proper meat for children of that age."

"Don't you think the headmaster knew enough about his job to keep things on the right level?"

"It wasn't Henry Gower's level that worried me. It was the level at which they themselves interpreted things."

"What do you mean?"

"I mean that you have to be careful what ideas you put in front of children—even when you're trying to teach them the differences between good and evil."

"There are a lot of people who'd like to see more of that done—with a bit more emphasis on black here and white there."

"I'm not against that," Patsy Price said, arguing now as if she and Kenworthy were equals. "But you have to keep the issue simple. All this talk of making pacts with the Devil—"

"You're not suggesting that they've been taking that seriously?"

"It must have crossed their minds. It can't *not* have crossed Davina Norris's mind. And she's never been slow at cross-fertilizing the others. I've got a feeling, Mr. Kenworthy, that there was something very unhealthy indeed going on at those secret meetings in the pumping station. And I don't think it was the script of Gower's play that they were reading over. Anyway, I'm getting far too far away from the subject—"

"It sometimes pays to do that. Sometimes that's the only way of seeing new light on it. But you haven't said much about the Parbolds' reaction to Elsie Frost's confession."

"Nigel Parbold wasn't prepared to accept Elsie Frost's word about anything. Not without a lot of investigation, he said. Didn't I think it had been bullied out of her—or coaxed into her? So that there wouldn't have to be a court case?

"I told him that obviously we had to take it seriously, consider it from all angles. And I think this was the first time he saw what it meant in terms of his own family discipline."

" 'You mean that all the complaints against Henry Gower were wilfully composed—and that Karen had been as deeply involved in these false accusations as the rest of them? I refuse to believe it.'

"I'm afraid I left them in mental and emotional chaos," WPC Price said.

·7·

NORRIS: DAVINA CATRIONA
(Source: Records of St. Botolph's Fen End C of E
Primary School, Norfolk.)

Born Basildon, Essex. Age: 11.11.
Height 4ft. 6ins. Weight 7st. 2lb.
Hair blonde (tinted). Eyes blue. Small round scar (ex
chicken pox) above left eyebrow.
IQ 150 + * (Blouet Attainment Tests).
   *A footnote drew attention to the unreliability of
quotients in the upper median (styled "near genius").
Hobbies: Riding (owns pony, kept in paddock in Half
Moon Lane). Reading, drama and listening to pop
music. Plays recorder. Played parts of Angel, nativity
play (Infants), Innkeeper's Wife (Infants), Virgin Mary
(Years III, IV & V), Prologue and Presenter (Year VI).
Title speaking role in *Fausta*, also cooperated on
script, wardrobe, scenery.

Athletics: Winner, egg and spoon race (Infants, Year
I), high jump (Year IV). Learned to swim, one width
(Year I), two lengths (Year II).

Attended School Camp (Years IV, V & VI).

A highly intelligent, outgoing child who takes a lively
interest in everything that comes her way. Naturally

takes the lead in a wide variety of activities. Has intense intellectual curiosity and extraordinary powers of perseverance.

Note by Gwynneth Ellis, Class Teacher
Has moods. Liable to sulk if relegated to second-rank activity, though can recover with remarkable resilience, or may go on resenting correction for days. She is best brought round by being allowed to shine at some new activity, whereupon she appears to harbour no ill feeling, and even to forget what had previously gone wrong.

"Mrs. Norris didn't want to cooperate," Constance Kimble said.

" 'Don't you think I've had enough to contend with without being dragged through all this again?'

"I remember how she pleaded a hairdresser's appointment half way through the very first interview I had with her. She was always at her most fluent when I encouraged her to grumble about her lot in life—not that she needs encouragement. I just gave her her head. There's ample evidence about her house of an indulged existence—consumer durables, trendy decor, every kind of gadget imaginable. Resentment seems an ingrained habit with her. She was angry about the lasting after-effects on Davina of what Gower is accused of doing, but I don't think she'd given any real thought to the problem. She is a woman who likes limelight. She likes to stick to *in* forms. She talks a great deal in clichés."

"And I take it you have a theory about her discontent?" Kenworthy asked.

"Her husband for certain. He's frequently away from home, often for long periods. He's away at the moment—left last week for Indonesia, via Norwich Airport and Amsterdam. Before they settled in Norfolk, he was running a small mail order firm on an industrial estate on the edge of Basildon New Town. Mrs. Norris disclaims any knowledge of her husband's business concerns—or any interest in them, but I came away with a firm picture of the Basildon venture: under-capitalized, but with a glossy sales catalogue. Norris's method appears to have been to buy from wholesalers only after he'd received enough retail orders. So there were often delays in deliveries to customers. The business eventually ran down, which Mrs. Norris blames on late deliveries, unreliable sources of supply, bad debts and cash-flow problems. But although he failed in Basildon, he must have salvaged quite a bit from the wreck. Their house here cost more than a song and Norris had enough capital to launch himself immediately in speculative trading in commodity futures. And this—as far as his wife admits to knowing anything about his affairs—has been their main source of income since he brought his family to Norfolk. She believes that most of his travelling is concerned with making his own assessments of forthcoming harvests and market trends in all manner of goods: zinc, copper, copra, cocoa, raw materials for the pharmaceutical industry. He doesn't handle these products, rarely even sees them. They exist only as purchases and resales from and to men whom he has as often as not never met. Oh, and he keeps cash-flow problems at bay by investing on behalf of syndicates who have confidence in his superior knowledge. All of which information was forthcoming from a woman who repeatedly insisted that she knew nothing at all about her husband's business. She believed he had gone to Java because of something to do with quinine."

Kenworthy took Sergeant Parrott with him to call on Cynthia Norris. In a way he was as interested in this inscrutable, straight-limbed young sergeant of ladylike quality as he was in any of the principals in the action. What sort of a copper could Sergeant Parrott be? How on earth did she react to the pathetic scruffs she must spend the bulk of her time with on her squalid pre-teenage exercise? What the hell could they possibly make of her? Come to that, how was she reacting to bucolic Norfolk? She gave no sign that she was reacting at all. She said, when he asked her, that it was new territory to her, but she did not appear to be looking round her with any special curiosity. She showed neither interest nor scorn—not even physical distress at the appalling cold. There was a bitter north-easter cutting savagely across the unsheltered marshes, and her ungloved hands were blue, obviously numb. But she did not complain about that—not even comically.

As soon as Kenworthy saw the Norris household, he knew what Constance Kimble had meant about possessions and gadgetry. There was a sophisticated programmable video with a shelf of commercial VHS tapes, mostly montages by pop groups. There were patent watering devices stuck into her houseplant pots; a mock-up copper etching-plate of an old map of the county; a hand-painted plate depicting blue-tits and one displaying medieval crafts. It looked as if the Norrises started to collect every new series that came out, but had never persevered beyond the first issue. Cynthia Norris had only to see a thing to want it. Wanting it, she acquired it: her house was full of acquisitions for which she had found she had no use. Kenworthy also caught the whiff of gin on her breath—at this time in the morning—and wondered whether she was an alcoholic, or merely tiding herself over a crisis.

She was immaculately turned out, under a quilted pink housecoat. *Soignée* had to be the only word. Sexy? Kenworthy could not be certain: not throwing any of it at him, that was for sure. She looked sorry for herself, but then she must have passed a poor night. Kenworthy asked her (though he knew the answer) what the news was from the hospital. Davina had had a restful night. Mrs. Norris was standing by for news at this very moment, just as soon as the consultant had done his morning rounds. If there was anything positive, Kenworthy would understand that this interview would have to be cut short.

Of course.

They had offered for her to stay at the hospital overnight. But what would have been the point of that, the child being so heavily sedated? She shuddered when she remembered the offer to accommodate her in some sort of cubicle at the end of the ward. Cynthia Norris's first reaction to everything was to resent it.

And Polly Parrott's only reaction to everything seemed to be not to react.

Mrs. Norris did not know whether Davina kept a diary or not.

"I don't know what these kids do with half their time. Davina spends hours up in her room scribbling at something or other. But a diary? I suppose everybody keeps a diary at some time or other, don't they—for a day or two at the beginning of the New Year?"

Did she know much about where the girls got to on their wanderings?

"Oh, Lord, I don't know. They don't tell us much of what they get up to. They spend a lot of time at each other's houses."

"Don't you worry about them when they're out of doors?"

"Worry? I used to worry myself stiff, when we first came to live here. I'm not a country person by any manner of means. I don't even like crossing fields with cows in them. But kids seem to develop a sense of self-preservation. That's the trouble, of course. That's what's happened now. They're too trusting."

"Did Davina ever say anything about an old pumping station?"

"Pumping station? I know the place you mean. Filthy old ruin. Ought to be restored or pulled down, one thing or the other. No. I can't say I ever heard Davina mention it. I've no doubt they've looked it over. St. Botolph's Fen End doesn't actually bristle with attractions and counter-attractions."

"If I might have a look at some of Davina's books and papers, Mrs. Norris—"

"I really don't know where she keeps anything. Her drawers and cupboards are always in a mess."

"She can't have an unlimited amount of belongings."

"I don't know whether we ought—"

"This is now a murder inquiry, Mrs. Norris."

"I'd like to help you all I can, Mr. Kenworthy. But I don't see what you hope to find out from anything of Davina's. You people are for ever treating Davina as a criminal. She isn't, you know. She was a victim. In any case, don't you have to have a search warrant, to take papers away?"

She seemed vague. Why did she bring up the subject of a search warrant? Kenworthy presumed she had heard vaguely about search warrants, perhaps on TV. Presumably she had some vague idea of standing on her rights. Or maybe there were papers of her husband's that wouldn't bear prying into.

"I could get a warrant for the asking—but we don't want all that palaver, do we? That isn't the spirit in which I've come here."

Kenworthy moved towards the stairs and Mrs. Norris followed, indecisive. There was something fundamentally weak about her: not a difficult woman to frustrate by a *fait accompli*. Kenworthy went into Davina's room. The child's incunabula—notebooks, folders, sheaves of loose papers, were on one of her lower shelves. He picked up a few of them, found as if by sure instinct what he was most hoping to find: a series of exercise-books in all colours and sizes, dating from her days in the infant class.

"Have you ever read any of these?"

Mrs. Norris shrugged without interest.

"I've glanced at them a time or two, when I've been cleaning. It's only kids' stuff. Kids have to develop, don't they? I never have believed in interfering."

"All these are ancient. I wonder where she keeps her more up-to-date bits and pieces?"

They ought not to be too difficult to find. The room was not large, and had few possible hiding-places. Kenworthy looked round systematically. Then Sergeant Parrott stepped forward and put her hand on a broken-cornered executive briefcase, no doubt one passed on by Davina's father. She picked it up, and Kenworthy heard its contents slide about inside: a book or two, and from the sound of them, some writing implements.

"I'm going to ask you if I may take this. I'll give you a receipt for it."

Mrs. Norris's tongue touched her lower lip, but any protest she was thinking of making sank back inside herself.

"I don't know what my husband will say."

"I expect you'll have these things back by the time you see him again. Tell Davina I'm looking forward to meeting her. I'm sure she'll be bounding about like her old self after a short rest."

He led Sergeant Parrott out into a world where the greenery was beginning to look as if the sap would soon be rising. There were times when a sight of greenery could be refreshing.

"Care to risk an assessment, Sergeant?"

Sergeant Parrott shrugged her shoulders.

"Bit early for that, I think. There are one or two questions I would have liked to ask."

"Why the hell didn't you, then?"

"Sorry—I wasn't sure—"

"Sergeant Parrott, much as I enjoy your delectable company, you are not here for purely ornamental purposes."

"I'll bear that in mind."

He stopped walking and cast his eye along a row of houses.

"Sex, for example. How would you rate Mrs. Norris as a sex kitten?"

"A disappointed one," Sergeant Parrott said. "Her husband's away, of course—"

"And I dare say she finds the opportunities for playing around in St. Botolph's somewhat circumscribed."

"I haven't had the chance to cast my own eye over the potential of St. Botolph's Fen End yet," Sergeant Parrott said.

*   *   *

In the hospital Davina Norris remained forbidden territory, at least, as her mother had said, until after the morning's rounds. The night-duty WPC handed over to her relief. There was nothing to report, only a barrier of nurses cheerfully jealous of their charge: no delirium, no talking in Davina's sleep. The ward sister rang Mrs. Norris before lunch to tell her that her daughter was to be allowed home that afternoon, but must be protected from harassment and was to have no visitors until her GP had seen her.

The first thing the child noticed when she arrived back in her bedroom was that her father's old briefcase was not in its usual place. When her mother told her what had happened to it, she went into a rage of a kind that Mrs. Norris had never witnessed before. She rang urgently for their GP, who came within half an hour and gave her a barbiturate hypodermically.

Kenworthy and Sergeant Parrott went next to the home of the Frosts.

"And don't forget—you're here to interrupt," Kenworthy said. "You say you know my reputation. Don't let it turn you into stone."

"The trouble is, you're not living up to it," she said.

He turned his head, so that she could not see him grinning.

And Sergeant Parrott gave another sign that she might have a sense of mischief.

"Maybe you're going to regret having issued this invitation, Mr. Kenworthy."

Bert Frost, as they had expected, was at work—in some distant field spraying winter wheat. Mrs. Frost had more to say than she had had when her husband was in the house, but she said it quietly, and under a sense of shame about her child's confession. It was true that there had been sex lessons at the school, but they had been unexceptionable in character, had not exceeded the limits of the sober little book which Henry Gower recommended annually to his

Parent-Teacher Association. It was true that the four girls had stayed behind one day at the end of the afternoon school to ask questions. But they had been unobjectionable questions, which the headmaster had answered factually. The outrageous accusations had been flagrantly untrue.

"It hasn't properly sunk in yet," Daisy Frost said. "And it still staggers me how much those girls know. They talked about what Henry Gower was supposed to have done as if he really had done it. They spend too much time talking to older girls. They're always hanging about the bus when it comes back from the secondary school—especially Davina and Karen."

"I'm afraid there's one particular topic of conversation that generally works its way to the top, even among children of that age," Sergeant Parrott told her.

"Well, it disgusts me. How can they ever be the same again?"

"By getting back to their normal lives as soon as they can. Of course you've got to beat the big drum about giving false evidence—but don't go on beating it for ever. Do you mind if I ask you a few pointed questions?"

"It's your job, isn't it?"

"What part did Elsie play in the puppet show?"

Kenworthy suppressed his surprise. He was not sure how Sergeant Parrott had got to know anything about the puppet show. He had not mentioned it to her.

"She was not one of the stars," Mrs. Frost said. "Her voice isn't strong enough. I'm afraid my Elsie is never in the front rank when it comes to public appearances. I never was myself."

"But she did take part?"

"Yes, everybody did—and not only the children. I can tell you a thing or two about that. It almost had me siding with the ones who are dead against all these capers. It must have been a sight easier for parents when the school day was all long multiplication and spelling. Mr. Gower used to say he was proud of involving the whole village. He certainly

involved me. I was sewing costumes for puppets well into
the small hours, the night before the dress rehearsal."

"So what was Elsie's contribution?"

"She painted scenery, sold programmes, played the
gramophone records in the intervals. And she spent hours
out of school, helping the others to learn their parts. I'm
sure she could have recited the whole script."

"There's one more thing I'd like to know. Is there any
particular place that you've told her to keep away from in
the last few months? Somewhere you didn't care for her and
her friends to go?"

The question clearly puzzled Mrs. Frost.

"I don't know what you mean. They've all always been
welcome in each other's houses."

"Lucky children. So has the word *trespassing* ever
cropped up?"

"Trespassing?"

Again, Daisy Frost saw no point in the question.

"Trespassing where? Where could they trespass in St.
Botolph's Fen End?"

"In the old pumping station?"

Elsie's mother reddened.

"Now you come to mention it, there was some talk about
the old pumphouse. That old busybody John Thurlow
stopped me in the street one morning and told me he didn't
think they ought to be playing there."

"When was this?"

"*When* was it?"

"Before or after the puppet show?"

Mrs. Frost could not be sure. She had probably not given
it another thought since Thurlow had spoken to her. She
looked in appeal to Kenworthy, for although he seemed to
be leaving the dialogue to this classy young woman, she
knew that he was the one in charge.

"Does this matter?"

"It could."

"How could it matter?"

"Sergeant Parrott is asking the questions," Kenworthy

said, not abruptly, but with an insistence that reminded Mrs. Frost of the harsh reality of the investigation.

"I suppose it was after the show, not before it. Yes—I'm sure it was. Mr. Gower had had us all working so hard in one way or another that everybody felt flat when it was over. The girls couldn't find anything to do with themselves the weekend after. I remember they went out for a nature-walk, said they were going to look for frogspawn. I told them it was much too early in the year. It was a chilly day, and I dare say they were glad of the shelter of the pumphouse."

"It strikes me, Mrs. Frost, that your daughter and her friends are just the types who'd keep diaries."

"They have to. Mr. Gower has them keeping diaries as soon as they can write. Elsie has kept a diary since she could put words together. Only last Christmas, the present she asked for was a five-year journal, complete with lock and key. I don't think she's missed a day, except when she's been ill. And even then, she's written something up afterwards."

"Mrs. Frost—if we could—"

But Mrs. Frost was uneasy about that idea.

"We've always had the clear understanding with Elsie—"

"Mrs. Frost—a man has been murdered."

"I'm sure you're not going to find anything about murder in my Elsie's diary."

"I don't suppose for a moment that we shall. But I think we shall very likely find something informative."

"I would feel I was letting her down, Sergeant Parrott."

"It will get us off on the wrong foot if I have to requisition it. I'd far rather she handed it over voluntarily. Can't you put it to her—say we need her help—promise her that we shall respect anything confidential?"

Mrs. Frost saw that that might be a way out—but she still did not want to make a decision here and now.

"I'll talk to her when she comes home from school."

* * *

"How do you come to know about the puppet show, Sergeant?"

"I heard some talk in the Report Centre, while you were going over documents."

"And you believe we ought to take these puppets seriously?"

"The play was a Henry Gower version of *Faust*."

"And?"

"As Mrs. Frost just said, even the adults were feeling deflated—and there were four eager young ladies desperate to be occupied. What if they thought of making their own compact with the Devil?"

"You're serious, Sergeant Parrott?"

"About compacts with the Devil—or about children who think of making them?"

"You mean they could believe in a thing like that?"

"It isn't only children who do. And they could have worked on each other's minds. These strike me as impressionable kids."

"Kids who played at evil?"

"You could say that what they did to Henry Gower came under the heading of evil, couldn't you? Things like that easily get out of hand."

"So now you're seeing the other end of your London picture," Kenworthy said.

"How do you mean, sir?"

"Couldn't any one of these four have wound up among your missing pre-adolescents?"

Sergeant Parrott shook her head emphatically.

"What I meet are the ultimate catastrophes, the outcome of boredom, of catastrophic experiments and despair. I meet callow imitation and a great deal of sheer silliness. I meet craziness over pop idols, sex, drugs and child prostitution. But evil in the abstract—that's something that hasn't come my way yet."

Kenworthy nodded appreciatively.

"I hope you're wrong. Henry Gower was crucified by

children—but it wasn't a child who took a knife to him. If
you want me to play guessing games as early as this, I'd say
someone took the law into his own hands. Perhaps it was
someone who saw him with Davina Norris yesterday
afternoon, then again in the evening—and rushed in to
protect her. But it's early days to be hobbling ourselves to
pet theories. And it'll do us both good to remember that
juvenile fantasies are dangerous ground."

"I think we may possibly be up against four very
dangerous girls, Mr. Kenworthy."

Chief Inspector Wilson asked Kenworthy how he wanted
his existing task-force deployed. Kenworthy told him to go
on covering their present angles until further notice.

So DC Dicky Warburton and PC Norman Purkis were set
on house-to-house inquiries in St. Botolph's and given a
target sector of the village to cover by lunch-time.

"If you're doing this for the first time," Wilson told
them, "you'll have learned a few lessons before this
morning is over. You'll find out that men and women often
have good reasons for not caring to tell you where they were
and who they saw last night. In nine cases out of ten, it will
have nothing to do with any crime. And even if what they
know could help us, they may do their best not to tell us.
They will argue that nothing they could pass on to us would
bring the victim back, whereas what they are hiding could
wreck their lives and somebody else's. So be on the
look-out for devious motives. Try to see through them. It
gets easier with practice. I'm not just thinking of people
who strayed into the wrong bed. Some chaps will bugger up
an inquiry rather than risk it coming to their wives' ears how
many pints they actually had last night."

• 8 •

DEAN: PAULINE ROYSTON
Born King's Lynn, Norfolk. Age: 11.6.
Height 4ft. 9ins. Weight 8st. 7lb.
Hair dark brown, cut in fringe. Eyes hazel.
IQ 128 (Blouet Attainment tests). (Significantly lower
score in six-monthly test after slow recovery from
glandular fever.)

Hobbies: Nature-study; reading; listening to pop music. Angel in Nativity Play (Infants). Took part in
crowd scenes Years I–IV. Behind-scene help with
Fausta.

Is no athlete. The only "standard" she ever reached
was in the long jump, 1981. Was the last in her year
group to learn to swim.

An overgrown, one can only say ungainly girl, whose
physical coordination is not always all that it might be.
Is apt to break things, e.g. objects made laboriously in
handicraft lessons. Has high average intelligence but
does not like the limelight until she is absolutely
certain of the activity concerned.

Note by Gwynneth Ellis, Class Teacher
A good-natured child, who would like to be in the
swim but very seldom is. She does not seem to resent

her backwardness in practical and physical things, but
would do anything to keep the friendship of those who
are good at them. Is therefore sometimes easily led
when she sees a hope of popularity. It is in some ways
a pity that she has to spend most of her spare time in a
group dominated by one particular personality.

Jack Dean opened the door to them. He was home for the
day, said this was not unusual, as when he was involved in
a new computer program he could work better away from
office interruptions. No one came out openly with the
suggestion that he was here to stay close to the core of
events in St. Botolph's Fen End.

Helen Dean was making a very credible job of appearing
cheerful: an educated woman who was still attractive after
fifteen years of marriage. Kenworthy was brisker with both
parents than he had been with anyone else so far, appearing
to treat them as businesslike people who he presumed spoke
the same language as himself.

"I want to know first whether your daughter has ever kept
a diary."

By way of answer, Dean produced it, already parcelled
and Scotch-taped, ready to be handed over. It was significantly less copious than Davina's.

"They all keep diaries at our village school. One of the
legacies of Henry Gower."

Kenworthy asked him if he had read it.

"I have."

"Uncomfortable reading, I dare say."

"That's the word for it, Chief Inspector. I won't say I'm
ashamed—I hope I have a more realistic scale of values than
that. But it would be easy to overreact. I admit that I'm
shaken. And puzzled, by more than one aspect of it."

His wife smiled thinly.

"This is the stage at which many parents would look hurt
and blank and say they don't know where they went
wrong."

"We have agreed, darling—there's no question of our having gone wrong."

"We've gone wrong by not knowing enough of what's been going on."

"You can't know what's going on in other people's minds—especially children's."

"You can know more than we did."

"This is not a very fruitful line of discussion," Dean said. "We can't alter the facts of the past. We can only try to get them straight in our minds so that we can try to organize the future. I'm sorry, Mr. Kenworthy. These are our problems. I hope you'll be able to find time to discuss them with us when you've read this diary for yourself. But I'd rather leave it until you have. And I have a very great favour to ask of you—though I've no wish to try to pre-empt you. I know that the inquiry ahead of you is going to be exacting."

Kenworthy inclined the ear of a courteous listener.

"Would you mind not questioning Pauline until you've gone through the journal? It will be easier for her to talk, once she believes that you know all the worst already."

Kenworthy made a play of feeling the weight of the packet in his hand.

"That makes sense. I don't think this will take me too long. And obviously, you'll do all you can to make sure she isn't afraid of talking to us."

"She's a good kid—but she's bound to be nervous."

"Yes. I can't help feeling that all four of them have something to be nervous about."

Detective-Constable Dicky Warburton and PC Purkis learned a great deal from their knocking at the doors of St. Botolph's. They learned, for example, that Mrs. Sarah Ballard had had a letter this morning from her son in the Gulf. They were pressed to read that letter. They went from Mrs. Ballard to Mrs. Crabtree next door and to Mrs. Lovell across the way, always on the lookout for the symptoms of which Chief Inspector Tom Wilson had warned them. But no one aroused their suspicions that they might have anything to hide about their movements last night. No one they had spoken to so far appeared to have indulged in any movements last night. They had all been indoors watching the Two Ronnies on television. And since they were still laughing and could regurgitate whole chunks from the sketches, they all appeared to be telling the truth.

Warburton and Purkis went on to the next on their list: *Sheriff* John Thurlow. And it was obvious before Thurlow even asked them into his house that here was a man unlike the others. John Thurlow's house, like Hannah Maslin's, was one of the few cottages in the village that had remained unimproved. John Thurlow, who looked to be in his late forties, lived in it with his aged, mentally confused, bedridden and incontinent mother. He did not go out to work, except to do odd jobs that the Inland Revenue did not know about. He was paid some sort of allowance by the DHSS so that he could stay at home and look after the old woman. St. Botolph's in general agreed with this policy: it took less from the public coffers than putting her into a home—and he was said to be very good to the old girl.

Warburton and Purkis did not know any of this the first time they called. They only knew what they saw and heard. They saw a hitching-rail, made from old poles, outside the Thurlows' back door. They saw a rope hanging in a lynching noose from an apple-tree in the small garden. When they went into the Thurlows' kitchen, they saw Thurlow's gunbelt and chapparals hanging on the door, his Stetson on a peg above them. On the table was a plate smeared with the remnants of bacon and beans. Thurlow was wearing a lumberjack's tartan shirt with a silver star made from foil pinned over the breast pocket. There was a pile of tatty paperbacks on the windowsill, all of them Westerns. Pride of place in the small bookcase was a glossy *Time-Life* series about the heyday of trail-drivers, gunmen and bounty-hunters.

Warburton went and examined the revolver in its holster on the door. It was a convincing but unbored replica of a Colt .45.

"Mr. Thurlow?"

"As on my baptismal susstificate."

If they had been led to expect the racy drawl of a cattlemen's saloon, they were disappointed. Thurlow made no attempt at the cowboy vernacular. He talked in a quiet voice, with West Norfolk vowels in the West Norfolk rhythm.

"I expect you'll know what we're here about, Mr. Thurlow."

"I expect I do."

"We're making inquiries throughout the village, trying to find anyone who noticed anything unusual yesterday evening."

"There I'm afraid I can't be any help to you."

"How did you spend the evening?"

"I listened to the radio—we don't have the telly—and I read this."

He picked up and showed them a novel by J. T. Edson.

"You didn't go out at all?"

"Not at all."

"You didn't see anything unusual from your window?"

"I didn't look out."

"You didn't hear anything?"

"Nothing that I don't hear every evening."

An old cheap clock chimed tinnily on the mantelpiece. A garden bird flew up against the back window, assaulting his own reflection.

"But there's something I *can* tell you."

"Yes?"

John Thurlow went off into a catalogue of the woes that had befallen St. Botolph's Fen End since the withdrawal of their resident policeman. He also compared today's school discipline with what it had been in his day. And he blamed the pollution of society on the media. He used the word *media*. His conversation was almost entirely a *réchauffé* of other people's talk.

DC Warburton concluded the visit as quickly as he

reasonably and decently could. Outside he looked at the Electoral Roll from which they were working.

"Who's next?"

"A Mrs. Hannah Maslin."

"It'll be the same all over again, I expect."

•9•

KENWORTHY WAS ITCHING to get at the diaries but he needed solitude, and solitude in St. Botolph's Fen End was hard to find. The arrangements as at present improvised in the Village Hall did not provide him with a corner in which he could be private. Even if they had, there would have been a queue of people waiting to share his privacy with him—people curious to meet a Yard man in the flesh, policemen anxious to let their diligence be seen.

Kenworthy tucked the diaries under his arm and walked towards the northern exit from the village. He heard footsteps behind him, knew that he was being followed. He dodged into a telephone-box, flicked over the page of the directory so that he could look back, saw that Constance Kimble was coming after him, though still on the far side of the road. He knew then that he had impulsively made a bad tactical error. He had bottled himself in. She had only to come and wait outside the door of the kiosk, and she had him where she wanted him.

Then he saw a slow-moving tractor, drawing a trailer spilling dung, about to pass. For five seconds it was between Connie and the kiosk, and in that vital space of time, Kenworthy was out of the booth and standing back behind a high corner of hedge at the inlet of a gate. He pictured Connie looking bewildered up and down the road: she had only to step three yards and she would be upon him.

But she didn't. She made a bad choice and walked instead a short distance along the road down which the tractor had come. There was a row of labourers' cottages there, and perhaps she thought he had gone to call at one of them.

Then he heard a woman laugh. She was standing at the gate where he was hiding—a woman in her early forties, her badly dyed blonde hair mostly concealed under a tight print headscarf, intended to hide her curlers. Her eyes were obviously smarting from the smoke of the cigarette between her lips.

"I'm going to ask you a favour, ma'am. You know who I am?"

"I can guess."

Not Norfolk speech. Not a local woman. A Londoner. Spitalfields or Hackney. Kenworthy felt a sharp nostalgia, as if he had been away from home for years rather than hours.

"I need somewhere uninterrupted, where I can look over some papers."

She pulled the gate open for him. Connie was likely to put her nose down this lane at any moment.

He followed the woman into her house, and she showed him to a corner in a sitting-room that smelled of mildew. Its fireside carpet was totally occupied by an upturned lady's bicycle.

And so at last he was alone with the daily recorded doings of Davina Norris and Pauline Dean. Davina's diary had started in the earliest days when she was beginning to learn to write. That seemed to be Gower's teaching policy.

"Mummy took me shopping in King's Lynn on Saturday."

Obviously the first entries had been copied from models provided by the teacher.

"I came to school this morning in my birthday present scarf. It has green and yellow stripes."

But it had not been long before Davina struck out independently, as evidenced by the abandon of her early spelling.

"Dammed television broke down again tonight, only to
minuets after the beginning of *The Increddable Hulk*.
Rote to the NSPCC today because she still has not
given me last week's pocket money."

She had not been more than six and a half when she had
written that. Kenworthy leaped ahead to more recent
events—not mere pages ahead, but skipping over a whole
pack of exercise books. Davina's diary had soon started to
play a considerable role in her life: she had grown accus-
tomed at a very early age to having a confidant, and a habit
had quickly become a need. There was hardly a day without
an entry, and sometimes she extended herself to as much as
ten pages. Kenworthy thumbed the leaves to find February
23rd, the day of the allegations against Henry Gower.

"We stayed behind in school this afternoon and asked
Mr. Gower some questions that our book doesn't seem
to explain properly. We did not want to ask in class,
because boys with dirty minds like Stanley Andrews
would think it was a joke.
Mr. Gower looked surprised when I said that I could
not picture what a man's erection looks like. Grownups make a fuss about always giving us true answers to
anything we ask, but when it comes down to brass
tacks, Mr. Henry Gower is as bad as the rest of them.
He was embarrassed—it was most amusing. You could
see he was thinking hard about it. I am almost tempted
to say you could smell his brain smouldering. He
reached for a piece of paper, and picked up a ballpoint,
and I thought to myself, 'He's going to do a drawing
like the one on the boys' lavatory wall.'
Then he pushed the paper away, and you could see he
was thinking some more. Then he said, 'Come with
me into the stock-room. It would be better not to let the
whole world see what we are doing. Some people are
terribly stuffy about things like this.'
So we followed him into the stock room and I could

not help noticing that he dropped the catch of the lock after he had shut the door behind us. Then he unbuttoned his trousers and brought his thing out, and what a horrible object it is, all blue and shiny at the top. And I thought to myself, those two disgusting little brats of his must have come out of there in the first place. No wonder they look as if they have something missing. He told us to touch it, and I was surprised that he flinched a bit when I did. Then he touched me down there and said, 'Look, you flinched too, didn't you?' Karen touched him very gingerly and took her hand away again quickly. It reminded me of once when she was frightened of touching a toad, and was trying to pretend that she wasn't.

'Go on!' he said. 'It won't bite you!'

But Elsie would not touch it at all. She hung back and said afterwards that it made her feel sick. I suppose I ought to feel sorry for her. It's made me feel sick often enough, just looking at her.

We watched it throb and grow and he made us feel how hard it was now. And I said I wouldn't want a thing like that pushed into me, and he said that was different, those were special occasions, and you had special feelings when they happened to you.

What a day!"

Only then did Kenworthy catch sight of the last line of the previous day's entry:

"Tomorrow!"

So they had had it planned in advance—

He laid Davina's journal aside and picked up Pauline Dean's version.

"We stayed behind after school and asked Mr. Gower some questions that we did not understand in the book."

Her writing did not have the same confident fluency as Davina's, and she made an occasional mistake in spelling and punctuation.

"We did not want to ask him in school-time because boys like Stephen Andrews would have laughed—
We thought at first that Mr. Gower was only going to do a drawing for us. We can see those on the wall of the boys' yerinal any time we want—
Mr. G flinched when D touched him, and he touched her down there and said that she had flinched too.
When his thing had grown big, we had to feel how hot and hard it was.
I didn't like touching it, but Davina and Karen and I did. But Elsie wouldn't—"

Kenworthy's hostess chose that moment to come in with a coffee for him: actually Camp—with chicory: another experience from a previous existence that he thought he would never relive again.

"That's a good idea," she said.

"What is, Mrs.—?"

"Jeffs. My friends call me Maisie."

"My name's Kenworthy."

"I know."

"What's a good idea, Maisie?"

"Getting down to it and seeing what the kids themselves had to say. I'll bet you've got some good stuff there."

"Extremely interesting."

"I'll bet. My kids went to that school. Myself, I don't hold with the way they do things nowadays."

"No?"

"Still didn't know their seven times, when they went to the big school at King's Lynn. But they knew all that goes on on a stud farm. Because Mr. Gower took them to one, to see it all happening."

Then there was somebody at Mrs. Jeffs's front door. Her house was an odd mixture of ceramic ducks flying across the wallpaper, a small black and white TV and the damned bicycle that took up most of the space in this room. But she did run to chime bars.

It was Sergeant Parrott, asking if he was here.

"Well run to earth, Sergeant!"

"Not too difficult, since half the village seem to have seen you come in here. In any case, it's always been impressed on me that a sergeant's first responsibility is to be able to lay her hands on her Chief Inspector. There are three things, Mr. Kenworthy."

"One?"

"Connie's complaining that you don't seem to want to give her anything to do."

"I need to get a sense of direction myself first. Two?"

"Superintendent Blane, the big white Norfolk chief, is coming over at lunch-time. Everybody seems to like him. He has a reputation for sanity and soundness."

"That's going to make some of us stand out a mile."

"Finally, there's this for you. From the hospital."

A small buff envelope, marked *Strictly Private,* and addressed to Kenworthy personally. He tore it open.

"My God!"

He passed it for the sergeant to see.

"My God!" she echoed.

And her eye wandered down to the open diaries.

"Confirming the general impression, are they?"

"Very vivid narrative. Strong command of detail. Whichever of us next goes to the Norrises' must look out for what sex manuals they have in the house. I think you'll find there everything that Davina knows."

"And that she passed on to the others?"

Kenworthy picked out one or two key passages, made bookmarks from slips of paper and passed the books to Sergeant Parrott.

"Take a quick look at these bits. See if your impression is the same as mine."

She read rapidly, and handed the books back to him.

"They both quote precisely the same details, in the same

order—to the exclusion of all others. There are no individual variations—no personal impressions. And there would
be, if this had been genuine."

"Davina's diary provides the skeleton of the complaint
they first made about Gower—the statement that Inspector
Kimble could not break them on. These two accounts were
written from a scenario—whose originating genius was
obviously Davina. I dare say she dictated the same pattern
to the other two as well."

"This is fiendish, you know, sir."

"One fiend and three followers, possibly, you think? We
must get our hands quickly on the other two diaries. May I
leave that to you, Sergeant? I have a lot more work to do on
these."

"One thing I don't understand—" she began to say, then
hesitated.

"What don't you understand, Sergeant?"

"You've been a lot more tolerant than I would have been,
about those other two diaries," she said.

"In order to be seen to be tolerant, Sergeant. We are
going to need all the good will we can inspire, by the time
we tie pink ribbon round this file."

· 10 ·

HANNAH MASLIN KEPT Warburton and Purkis waiting at her back door. But when they started wandering about her yard and peeping into her outhouse, she came lumbering out.

"What do you want in there?"

"Just looking to see if there's anyone at home."

"You don't think I live in my shed, do you?"

She did not ask them in and did her best to keep her door as narrowly open as possible. They caught a glimpse of her living-room. It looked as if she might be having a cooking morning, but the dominant aroma was a rancid fat.

"We are police. You'll have heard that a man was killed in this village last night. We need all the help we can get."

"You'll get no help from me."

"Those that are not for us are against us."

"You'll get no help from me for the simple reason that there's no help I can give you. I've not set foot outside this house these last ten days."

Nevertheless, they took note that she showed no surprise at the news of the murder. Therefore she must have talked to someone since last night. Warburton was now obsessed by the need to penetrate into Hannah Maslin's house—by invitation.

The close proximity of her body was no more attractive to him than it would be to anyone else of normal human susceptibilities. He was nauseatedly aware of coarse skin, grime-clogged pores and several decades of elderly female sweats and exudations. But he now had one foot in the room.

"That looks like an interesting morning's work, Mrs. Maslin," he said, indicating the herbal paraphernalia on the crowded table. "What are you up to? Making illicit liquor?"

She looked at him with hatred. He did not underestimate the passion behind it.

"My lawful occasions," she said. "That's all you need to know about my business."

He read the labels on two of her jars. Valerian—believed by some to be a remedy for sleeplessness. Yarrow: reputed to bring relief in some forms of backache.

"Do you happen to know anything for boils?" he asked her. "I've got a beauty ripening up in a place I wouldn't care to show you."

She looked at him with no lessening of her hostility, perpetually on guard against mockery.

"I'm not kidding," he said, "and the last one I had was a right bugger."

"Steam in a bottle," she said. "Suck the core out of it."

"That's too bloody cruel. I tried it once. Thought I was going to end up inside the bottle myself."

He and Purkis were now both in the room.

"Do you get a lot of them?" she asked him, weighing him up now with professional eyes. "Boils?"

"Too many."

"Too much rich food. It's no use coming to me for a cure if you want to live on bottled sauces. I'll give you some ointment, if I've any left. And take a daily dose of soot from up the chimney—a teaspoon a day."

"That makes sense. Carbon clears poisons out of the blood. I think I'd prefer it in the form of charcoal biscuits, though."

"Please yourself. If you can afford to pay for what you can get free."

She rummaged clumsily among her miscellany of containers and came back with a pot of some sticky black substance, of which she scraped a helping into a small circular pill-box.

"Use this morning and night, and as often in the daytime

as you can find time and place to put it on," Hannah Maslin said. "I know it's not too easy in company when it's on your arse."

Warburton brought a pound note out of his wallet and gave it to her. She looked at him as if he were making a nuisance of himself, wheezed over and fumbled a fifty-pence piece out of a cabinet drawer.

"I always tell people to give what it's worth to them—but there's no need to overdo it."

Then Warburton understood something else. They were not the only ones who urgently needed information. So did Hannah Maslin. It was she who asked the next question.

"So you know who it was, then, who followed the girl down Mill Lane?"

"I do not. Do you?"

"No. I do not. But I know he was the reason the school-master followed them."

"You were watching, were you?"

"I'm not saying I was, and I'm not saying I wasn't."

"Mrs. Maslin, we haven't time to play games."

He had not meant to speak to her as harshly as those words came out. But he was surprised at the effect that they had on her. Instead of snapping back at him, it seemed as if she needed his goodwill as much now as he needed hers.

"Young man, don't take on at me like that. I'm trying to tell you the truth."

"Where were you watching from?" he asked her in softer tones.

She nodded her head towards her strategic curtain.

"People would be surprised at what I can see from my little corner."

"I'm sure they would. And what did you see yesterday evening?"

"I saw what I saw."

"Mrs. Maslin—"

"I can't tell you who it was, because I don't know. I saw the schoolmaster on his bike. I've felt sorry for him all along, though things would have been different if he'd acted differently. Everything that's happened, he's brought on to himself. He should have stuck to the old ways of doing things. But he was no match for those girls. Wicked girls."

"Why do you call them wicked?"

"Because I see what I see."

"Well go on, then, tell us—what have you seen?"

Warburton had decided that deep down she was dying to tell them, but not at his bidding—and certainly not at his nagging. She was not prepared to be clay in his hands. She had to speak of her free will, on her own terms.

"I saw this man come down the village, and he turned down Mill Lane. The girl came down a minute or two after him, just as the schoolmaster was coming home on his bike. She went down Mill Lane, and I thought she did that to keep out of his way. But he spotted her and went after her."

"And you don't know the first man?"

"I'm not going to say his name because I don't know for sure. If I was sure, I mightn't keep it from you. But I'm not sure. Thou shalt not bear false witness against thy neighbour. It was death by stoning, in Bible days, for giving false evidence. If I say his name, a man might be in trouble who's done nothing to be in trouble for."

"He was one of your neighbours then, you think?"

"You're not going to trap me like that, young man."

You could call her as wrong-headed as she was physically uncouth—but her staying-power was not going to be broken in minutes.

"If I ever find out—beyond any shadow of doubt—then I might tell you. But the light was bad. He had his back to me. I couldn't lean further out without being seen by half the village. I can tell you he's not the one that she's been seeing of an evening this last week or two."

"Seeing of an evening? Who's she been seeing of an evening?"

Hannah Maslin considered, then took the plunge.

"Simon Lovell."

"Who's Simon Lovell?"

"He goes to the big school. In King's Lynn. She's always

hanging round waiting for the bus when it comes back in the afternoon."

"How old is this laddie?"

She did some sum in her head, matching landmarks in village and family history.

"Thirteen, rising fourteen."

"How long has this been going on?"

"These last few weeks."

"And they've been meeting in the evenings? Every evening?"

"I can't say every evening. Most days. About seven. On the corner. Sometimes she keeps him waiting. On purpose. I know she keeps him waiting on purpose."

Warburton looked out of the window, assessing Mrs. Maslin's field of view.

"I'm not saying," she said, "that there's anything wrong in a lad meeting a lass. Except for this one being what she is."

"And what would you say she is, Mrs. Maslin?"

"A young madam. Too young for any boy at that school. I know they grow up early these days—though I was working full time when I was her age. But she could run rings round young Lovell—not that I've anything against him. But when I've seen them together I've asked myself: What's she wanting with him? She's got four times his brains—more's the pity. What can be worse than a mixture of brains and badness? If she's spending her time with Simon Lovell, it's not to swap Bible stories."

"Where did they go together, then? The weather hasn't exactly favoured courting evenings, this last month."

"The pumphouse, I suppose. That's the way they've always gone. Where else?"

"I don't know," Warburton said. "Where else is there? I've never done any courting in St. Botolph's."

"Are you a married man?" she asked him suddenly.

"Nowhere near married."

"But you have a young lady friend?"

"Several."

"Get yourself settled and regular," she said. "That would do your boils more good than half a ton of ointment."

"There is one more question, Mrs. Maslin. Last night: did Simon Lovell come out to meet Davina Norris?"

"I didn't see him."

"But she came out at her usual time, as if she were meeting him?"

"Round about then. Yes: it wouldn't be far off seven."

"You never told me you had a boil on your arse," Norman Purkis said, as they came out of Hannah Maslin's gate.

"My arse is cleaner than a wally's whistle. But look where a boil on my bottom has got us."

Arnold Blane was a big man—one of those big men whom cuddlesome women are sometimes heard to say they would love to cuddle. He came in casually, a little before the lunch-time briefing session that Kenworthy had ordered. He would not, he said, be staying long, had a busy afternoon ahead of him. VIPs coming to Sandringham.

In effect, nothing was casual about the Detective-Superintendent except the appearances he cultivated. When he arrived anywhere "casually," it was because he did not want to appear to be interfering; he had done his interfering before people knew it had happened. He came across Kenworthy casually. He casually asked Kenworthy if he thought this was going to be a long job. Kenworthy replied that he thought it could go either way.

"You've got everybody gainfully occupied, I take it?" Blane asked—almost as if he had already casually heard of Connie's discontent.

"As a matter of fact, no. But everybody soon will be. I've been a bit slow making up my mind what gainful employment means in this case."

He showed Blane the communication he had had from the hospital.

"My God!" Blane said.

"I haven't said a word to anyone about it yet. I thought

I'd see if the morning brought in hints from any other source."

"And has it?"

"No."

"Bad. This is going to make for misleading suspicions all round the village. What have you got Connie doing?" Blane asked, changing the subject bluntly. "Don't underestimate her, Kenworthy. She's good. She can be very good. She'd be better still if it occurred to her to make anybody like her. She's a martinet—even tougher with herself than she is with others. Must have everything neat and properly in place. Well, there are worse faults. Also I dare say she'd prefer it if Patsy Price were not as bright as she happens to be. Not that Price knows everything yet. She needs experience, and she needs encouragement, which is something Connie all too often overlooks the need for. I'm mentioning this, by the way, in case you're likely to underemploy either of them."

"It's unlikely that I shall."

Blane attended the briefing session, drifting into a casual corner where some forgot his presence, and from which he did not make any suggestions.

First there was a progress report from the uniform team that was searching the field where Gower's body had been found. It was a short-winded report. There had been no progress.

Then Warburton gave an account of their still incomplete house-to-house pilgrimage. Warburton had a light touch, and advised anyone calling on Mrs. Maslin to plead a minor ailment. Kenworthy took due note of Simon Lovell.

Finally he reached the medical report on Davina.

"You'll not need me to remind you that at the end of February, when this case was no more than an indecent behaviour and assault charge, all four of them were discreetly established *virgo intacta*. I'm afraid that that is no longer true of Davina Norris. I expect most of you know from experience how exasperating the medics can be when they're trying to be careful. They do not care to commit

themselves. A hymen can be lacerated by anything from
horse-riding to masturbation. You know the things the
doctors look for: seminal traces, smears, foreign pubic hair.
They have found no such traces about Davina Norris. But
there is significant dilatation, some bruising. The inference
is that *if* she's had intercourse with a male, it was some time
ago: very shortly in fact after the date of the original
complaint against Gower, shortly, in fact, after the medical
examination that she had then. That puts it roughly during
the first week of this month. The state of the *ecchymosis*—
that's bruising, to you, DC Warburton—supports this."

There was a good deal of whispered comment.

"Has anyone heard anything positive about Davina's
carryings-on that might pinpoint us further?"

Only about the lad Lovell.

"I want nothing said about this until I give the word. I
don't want the public, and especially not the press, to get
wind of it at this stage. But keep your ears close to the
ground. Warburton and Purkis, I want you to carry on
encouraging folk to talk—about anything they want to talk
about. You men searching the field, go on searching: any
dropped object that might identify anyone who's been there
recently. I'd like Inspector Kimble and WPC Price to
remain behind."

He spoke to Patsy Price in her Inspector's presence. The
young policewoman listened with an obvious sense of
occasion.

"If it's OK by you, Miss Kimble, I'd like to use WPC
Price for some routine clearing up."

"By all means."

"Miss Price, get hold of this Lovell boy as soon as he
comes home on the secondary bus. Get everything out of
him that you can learn about Davina Norris. *Everything*.
You might have to work hard to get him going."

"Sir."

"Sergeant Parrott and I want to spend the afternoon
working on the diaries. It may seem a sedentary occupation,
but it's primary evidence. You must use your discretion

about what we'd care to be interrupted for and what we wouldn't."

"Sir."

And then he was left alone with Connie Kimble.

"This a nasty one, Inspector."

"Most cases have their nasty side."

"Women have been known to gossip, Inspector, and I expect that's as true in rural Norfolk as it is in the Mile End Road. I hate the word *challenge*—but do you think you could pump the women of this salubrious village about any man who might have been with Davina Norris—*without* arousing their suspicions that we think somebody has? I know this is a tough one."

"I'll do my best, Mr. Kenworthy."

But he could not tell what inner thoughts, if any, she had on the subject.

᛫11᛫

FROST: ELSIE
Born St. Botolph's Fen End. Age: 11.7.
Height 4ft. 5ins.; Weight 6 st.
Hair Chestnut. Eyes blue.
IQ 127 (Blouet Tests)

Hobbies: Reading, nature-study, listening to pop music. Played part of Angel in a nativity play (Infants). Small walking-on parts (Year II, III and IV). Very reticent about speaking in public, but will work hard behind scenes at any activity.

Attended school camp (Year IV) but suffered from home-sickness until penultimate day and refused to come in subsequent years.

A reticent child, intellectually capable of grammar school work, though would probably suffer emotional and social difficulties. Surprisingly befriended by Davina Norris and her friends. There is some tendency to poke repetitive fun behind her back, because of her strong Norfolk accent and rather old-fashioned, one might almost say old-maidish, ideas, but she seems quite happy to tag along with them.

Note by Gwynneth Ellis, Class Teacher.
Almost too conscientious at times. Slows down her

own work by obsessive rechecking. Needs to be more reckless. A misfit in a small group of friends—but without them she would probably have no friends at all.

Sergeant Parrott was unprepared for the state in which she found the Frost household. The father, not unexpectedly, was out at work. The mother's voice could be heard even from outside the front door. It sounded as if she had lost self-control.

"If you say that word again, I shall go out of my mind."

Elsie's voice was not strong enough to carry, but whatever she answered served only to intensify her mother's rage.

"You've brought this all on yourself. You've only yourself to blame if he does come for you."

Sergeant Parrott rang a second time, but still no one came. She tried the door and the latch was up, so she let herself quietly in. Mrs. Frost came towards her, spreading her hands in an unfinished gesture of hopelessness. She made no complaint about the detective's uninvited entrance. Perhaps she had been hoping that the caller would go away, but now she was here there was nothing she could do about it.

"Now look who's come for you."

An idiotic thing to say to a child who was already terrified by something. It was the first time that Sergeant Parrott had seen Elsie: she had pictured her as the most undersized, the most pinched and underdeveloped, the least active and the last athletic of the foursome. But it was shocking to see her now, sitting at the kitchen-table with a painting-book, which she had to all intents and purposes abandoned after her first failed smear of colour. She was chalkily pale, peaky, wild-eyed. She shrieked at the sight of a stranger.

"Mummy!"

It was a primæval appeal for protection, a reversion to the emotions of her baby years—triggered off by the arrival of

an unknown policewoman at the house. Did people still tell
their kids imbecilic scare stories about bogey policewomen?
It did not take Sergeant Parrott long to discover that Elsie
was petrified by notions that had nothing to do with the
police. But it might not have been her mother who had to
answer for this. Daisy Frost might only have worked
hysterically on what already existed. The child's fears came
largely from within herself.

"May I talk to her, Mrs. Frost?"

"For God's sake do talk to her. I wish someone would. I
can't get any sense into her. She's driving me out of my
wits. I can't stand any more of it. Have you come to take her
away?"

Mrs. Frost's eyes were as wild as her daughter's. God
knows how long she had been going hammer and tongs at
the child like this.

"I've told her she doesn't belong to me any more."

The woman seemed unable to open her mouth without
making matters worse. She must have given up all hope of
re-establishing any rapport with the girl, hated her because
of her own inability to enter her mind; was probably even
wishing that the child hadn't a mind. Mrs. Frost was
actually wringing her hands, like a stock character from bad
melodrama. How to keep a balance between the essentials
of the case and the normal decencies of human sympathy?
Sergeant Parrott was even beginning to feel uneasy at the
thought of this pair being alone in the house together.

"Mrs. Frost, has your doctor seen Elsie today?"

"Doctor? It isn't a doctor she needs—she's not ill."

"I think you should get him. At least he'll be able to
quieten her down. Would you like me to ring the surgery?"

And as soon as he set eyes on the mother, he would surely
put her under at least mild sedation as well.

She did ring the surgery. She had to go to the village
kiosk to do so. Mrs. Frost seemed unaware that she had
gone out of the house. The doctor was out on his rounds,
and it did not seem that they would be able to get a message
to him until he came in again at some unspecified hour.

"Is there a neighbour who would come in and give you a hand with things?"

"Oh God, no! I couldn't let anyone see us in this state. I don't know how I shall look anyone in the face again. I wish I could get away from here—from everything and everybody."

"Would you like me to make us all a coffee?"

And perhaps look round the house to see if there was a tot of anything stronger to offer her? But it wasn't the fashion to use spirits to stimulate people these days, was it?

"No—Yes—No—No. If you'd like a coffee, I'll make some."

It seemed a good thing for her to find something for her hands to do. Sergeant Parrott went and sat down at the table beside Elsie. The child was actually trembling. She cringed as the sergeant leaned towards her.

"Elsie, why are you frightened of me?"

Mrs. Frost made instant coffee in ordinary teacups.

Elsie did not answer the sergeant, would not even look at her.

"What do you imagine I am going to do to you?"

No reply.

"Elsie, I know and you know that terrible things have happened."

From the point of view of a sensitive child, lacking adult understanding, those terrible things must pass the threshold of tolerability. A schoolmaster was dead—a schoolmaster once dearly loved—the man who had been the centre of her life—the man she would have done anything to please—dead because of a disgraceful prank in which she had played a leading part. And all that filth was uncovered—all that history of obsession with lavatory-minded sex was being made public—in addition to a mother who had gone over the top about it.

Behind her, Sergeant Parrott heard Daisy Frost making an unnecessary rattle with her teacups.

"Elsie, you have nothing whatever to be afraid of."

If the child had tossed her head, it would have been

something. At least it would have been a rejection of grownups' blarney. But Elsie did not even rise to that.

"Elsie—I know and you know that there are things that you wish you hadn't done. I hope that there are some things that you wouldn't do again—ever."

She knew she sounded like an evangelizing moralist of the old school, but she saw no other way of conveying a message of hope. It produced no reaction.

"Elsie—"

Elsie's mother came over with the coffee, unnecessarily carrying the cup on a tray.

"Elsie—"

Sergeant Parrott felt her temper rising. Within control, that might not be at all a bad thing.

"Elsie, I'm not going to let you sit there much longer, refusing to answer me."

If the child did not pick up the danger signals in her tone, then it was difficult to know what might affect her.

"I know and you know that you've been a donkey—haven't you?"

Reducing it to childish terms might make it easier for her to face.

"Haven't you, Elsie?"

Silence. Polly said the words again, more gently.

"You've been a donkey—haven't you?"

The answer was no more than a sniff—but a sniff was a sort of answer. It was an acknowledgement not only that she had heard, but that she knew that she could not disagree.

"And you aren't going to be a donkey any more, are you?"

Elsie shook her head—still without meeting Polly's eye.

"Well, I'm glad we agree about something," Polly said cheerfully. "Because now we can begin to think about what we're going to do next."

No response from Elsie—not even given away by her eyes. Fear was still the strongest emotion in them.

"Let me put it this way: you and your friends have done

things you're not proud of. It isn't necessarily the end of the
world—"

Except for Henry Gower—

"You'd give anything now, not to have done those things.
Wouldn't you? Wouldn't you, Elsie?"

Elsie nodded.

"Let's be honest, Elsie. There are some things that can't
be put right. But there are still things we can do to help to
make amends. Do you know what making amends means?"

"Yes," Elsie said.

Daisy Frost seemed a little more settled. She was paying
close attention to what was being said.

"Tell me, Elsie. What does making amends mean?"

"It means putting things right you've done wrong."

A tiny, faraway voice—but a voice.

"Well, one way in which you can make amends is by
doing everything you can to help me. To help me to find out
who did that terrible thing to Mr. Gower. You'd want to do
that—wouldn't you?"

It was only by the slightest signal of facial expression that
Elsie said she would.

"I want to see your diary, Elsie."

"No!"

It was more than a refusal. It was a scream of finality—
the condemned prisoner trying to shout away the execu-
tioner.

"Why are you so determined that I should not see it,
Elsie? There's nothing in it that's likely to shock me. I spent
most of my life dealing with awful people—people much
more awful than you could ever imagine."

Elsie started to cry. "You'll put me in prison," she said.

"Elsie, we do not send little girls of your age to prison.
And it isn't a crime against any law in this land to write
anything you want to write in your own private diary."

It could be a different matter, of course, if one's parents
got hold of it. For a moment the image flickered across
Sergeant Parrott's mind of what would have happened if her
own father and mother, snug in the Beaconsfield stockbro-

ker belt, had found she had written a personal history like Davina Norris's.

"I can promise you that nothing will happen to you because of anything you have written in your diary. And I know that your mother will make you the same promise. Won't you, Mrs. Frost?"

Some such promise might be a way of temporarily patching things up between mother and child. Sergeant Parrott turned to look at Mrs. Frost, who nodded—grim-mouthed, but definitely more composed than she had been half an hour ago. Then, without saying where she was going or why, she turned abruptly and left the room. Sergeant Parrott heard her go upstairs.

"None of us are your enemies, Elsie."

And here was the chance to check on another vital point.

"I'm right, aren't I, Elsie—all four of you have kept diaries?"

"M'm."

"Including Karen Parbold?"

"Yes."

"You're sure about that?"

"Karen won a prize for hers in Mrs. Ellis's class."

"Do you mean to say that your teacher used to read your diaries?"

"Not after we went into Mr. Gower's class. He said we were too grown-up for that now."

Little did he know what the word *grown-up* might signify.

But if it sounded as if Elsie had found a new fluency, she reverted at once to her more familiar attitude the moment her mother appeared. Because of the way they were sitting, she saw her before Sergeant Parrott did.

"Mummy—no!"

Mrs. Frost was carrying a handful of exercise-books. They could only be Elsie's diaries.

"Mummy—no!"

"Take them, Miss Parrott. Do you know what's really the matter with her, Miss Parrott? She thinks the Devil is going to come for her—all because of some silly paper they're supposed to have signed. If I've told her once, I've told her a thousand times that there's no such thing or person as the Devil. Do you think you could get that into her mind?"

It was occasionally asserted in the CID Room—though perhaps not as an article of creed—that the Devil and his works were the gratifying source of their monthly salary cheques.

"I don't know whether there's a Devil or not, but I'm certain he's not interested in silly games that little girls play."

Elsie did not look comforted.

CHIEF INSPECTOR TOM WILSON was a believer in the Establishment. True blue labels on people gave him confidence. With Kenworthy's blessing he went to see the vicar of St. Botolph's Fen End before calling on Sheriff John Thurlow. The vicar turned out to be no true blue, but after a few minutes in his company, Wilson quite warmed to him. The Reverend Mike Palfrey was a latter-day throwback to the original muscular Christians. And he displayed refreshing realism about some of his parishioners.

"I can't say I'm surprised that Henry Gower ended up in trouble," the vicar said. "I'm sorry, of course, that it's taken the tragic turn that it has. And I never did believe that those girls were telling the truth. But he was a trifle too eager, a bit on the fast-moving side for rural Norfolk. He was always too ready to assume that people understood what he was getting at. That's a catastrophic failing in these parts."

"The man I really want to talk to you about is John Thurlow."

"Hopalong Cassidy, the Lone Ranger, Gene Autry, Buffalo Bill Cody and Wild Bill Hickock rolled into one. Quite harmless."

"But surely not quite right in his head?"

"He lives a fantasy life; which of us doesn't? I sometimes think I ought to admire John Thurlow more than I do. At least he has the guts to be open about his game-playing. But apart from the costume, it's all in his mind. He's not exactly

dull-witted—but not much above it. He doesn't make
himself a nuisance to anyone—at least, not with his
sheriffing. I've never even heard him talk to himself: there's
no clue as to what plots are playing themselves out all round
him. But he's also unfortunately a self-appointed keeper of
the village conscience—always stirring things up, in all
sorts of context. He's tried time and again to get up a
petition against our change-ringers. He takes strenuous
exception to our Romeos and Juliets who have nowhere to
copulate except in the open air. Most of them wouldn't be
seen, except by Thurlow, who goes out looking for them.
And he reports petty naughtiness out of school to the
teachers. Consequently he's quite often the butt of adolescent practical jokers. And now and then he has too much to
drink. It would happen more often if he could afford it.
Once or twice, when he's just received his Social Security
Giro, he's been stupidly generous in the pub, striving for
popularity. On the credit side, he's always been wonderful
with his mother. In the pub, when he's won a handful of
silver on the fruit machine, he'll buy a miniature brandy,
take it home to her, then come back to his pals. Not the
Brain of Norfolk, I'll admit—but I've never heard anyone
impugn his honesty."

"And sex? Is he quirky?"

"I've heard nothing adverse—except that he's an indig-
nant voyeur. I've never heard that people won't trust him
near children. I would think he's sexually more or less
dormant. He doesn't seem interested in women. I've never
heard that he has been—or that any woman has ever shown
interest in him. I'd have thought he was too grubby for
them—but I never cease to be surprised at what some
women seem to regard as a capture."

"Small boys?"

"Nothing's ever come to my ears."

"And what can you tell me about Mrs. Maslin?"

"Ah! That depends on whether she considers you friend
or foe. Foe, mostly—and her criteria defy analysis. She had
a fabulous knowledge of herbal cures—a legacy from her

mother. Old Hannah is grotesque—partly the victim of her physical frame. But she's let herself go, obviously never made the slightest effort to do anything about herself."

At this moment Palfrey's phone rang. Wilson wandered desultorily round the vicar's bookcases while he answered it. Palfrey was doing more listening than talking.

"This will interest you," he said when he had finished. "Old Dr. Swanson, our GP. Talking to me in confidence, you'll understand—but he'd be equally open with you. He's that sort of man. He's just been called in by Mrs. Frost. Have you met that family yet?"

"Not yet. This is my first working visit to your parish."

"I don't know the Frosts well. Nobody does. They're on my Parish Roll, but they don't come to church from one year's end to the next, and young Elsie has never been to Sunday School. It seems that now she's got herself into a terrible state. She believes that she and her friends have been in league with the Devil and that he's about to come to collect his dues. The old Doc wants me to go round and try to talk her into a healthier frame of mind. It's nice to have one's expertise known, isn't it?"

"I'll stay in touch," Wilson said.

Hannah Maslin had finished her day's dispensing when Kenworthy called. She had put away her jars and pestles but more than a suspicion of rancid fat remained in the atmosphere as testimony of her science. When Kenworthy knocked, she was sitting in her chair with a very ancient women's magazine open in her lap, and an even older pair of oval-lensed, nickel-rimmed spectacles about to slide off the end of her nose. They had belonged to her mother. Whatever her friend-or-foe criteria might be, Kenworthy did not measure up to them.

"Has some new law been passed, then, that a body's not to have her afternoon rest?"

"I'm sorry about this, Mrs. Maslin. But you've got to admit—unusual things have been going on."

"They have nothing to do with me."

"You were talking to two of my colleagues about a man you saw going down Mill Lane yesterday evening. Have you thought any more about that?"

"A lot."

"And what conclusion have you come to?"

"That I made a mistake."

"What sort of a mistake?"

"It was not the man I thought it was."

"Who was it, then?"

"I can't tell you."

"Mrs. Maslin, it is essential for us to know."

It was at this stage that Hannah Maslin's patience began to show signs of wear and tear.

"I can't tell you what I don't know, can I?"

"You mean that there's someone in this village that you don't know, Mrs. Maslin?"

"I don't know everybody."

"You mean it was a stranger to the village?"

"Isn't it a village of strangers these days?"

She went off then into a diatribe against the changes that had come over St. Botolph's Fen End—as if Fenland life had been idyllic in the days when ninety per cent of her neighbours had been casual labourers on the land—out of work and out of earnings whenever the weather was bad. School then had been slates, sums and the cane. On payday, women had had to waylay their men before they could get into the pub. Happy days; poverty, a sort of folk-poetry, community spirit and community suffering all scrambled by the whisk of Hannah Maslin's evil temper. Kenworthy decided that what she most held against the Norrises, the Deans, the Parbolds and the Frosts was that they had never been through what her generation had.

"What actual harm have these newcomers to St. Botolph's done you?" Kenworthy asked her.

"They've brought the likes of you round here, morning, noon and night, for one thing—getting me a bad name."

Kenworthy tried then to draw a description from her of

the man she claimed to have seen. But the old woman was
determined not to cooperate.

"Colour of his eyes? You tell me how I can tell the colour
of a man's eyes from the back of his head, on a dark
evening."

Kenworthy had lived long enough to recognize a waste of
time when he saw one. Bullying this woman would only
make her worse.

At her curtain, Hannah Maslin watched which way
Kenworthy went: down Mill Lane. Going to look at the
pumping station, no doubt. That suited her. She struggled
into her outdoor coat as if that in itself were a salutary act
of penance. She wheezed and tottered out of her gate and
waddled painfully up the village street. Such people as saw
her looked hard to assure themselves that it was true. It was
outside the pattern of St. Botolph's daily life for Hannah
Maslin to show herself in public in the middle of the
afternoon.

Tom Wilson made no progress with Sheriff John Thurlow.
It was not that Thurlow was truculent or even openly
resentful of another visit. He was simply morose. Whatever
else one thought about a man whose inner life was devoted
to Wild West fantasies, one hardly expected him to be dull.
But dull was what John Thurlow undeniably was.

Wilson, who had cheered his boyhood ration of goodies
in a Saturday Cinema Club, thought he might win Thurlow's approval with opening small-talk about the superiority
of *Rawhide* over Roy Rogers. But Thurlow's response
left him wondering whether he had ever heard of either
of them. The door from the tiny living-room-kitchen to
the diminutive front room was open, so that Wilson could
see a brittle and wispy old woman in a grey-sheeted and
unstable-looking bed. The house smelled of flaking old
age.

Wilson tried another approach. He fished for Thurlow's
admiration by broaching those matters of public scandal

against which he was said to wage one-man vigilante warfare: the sort of thing that went on on sultry nights behind the hedgerows of Mill Lane. John Thurlow looked back at him with clouded eyes, as if he did not know what he was talking about.

"So what can you tell me, Mr. Thurlow, about some of these kids at that school? A bit different from your school-days and mine, I'd say."

"Yes."

"Davina Norris, for instance. There weren't any girls like her in your class, I'll bet."

"There were girls in my class."

"Like Davina Norris?"

"Not like her."

But in what sense they had been different, he did not seem able to say. Tom Wilson persevered for a quarter of an hour, then concluded that he would be more usefully employed back at his Report Centre.

In the meanwhile, Hannah Maslin had transported her bulk the whole length of the village and had actually gone on beyond the parish limits to a long, straight lane where the red-brick Fenland cottages were strung out a quarter of a mile apart. On either side of her stretched flat fields, sodden still with the last of the winter's rains. A biting, briny wind from off the North Sea lashed her cheeks. Whatever Hannah Maslin suffered, she did not show it. But it was not for the astringency of fresh air that she had come as far as this. She had come past the Thurlows' cottage because she had seen in a glance through his window that the Sheriff had company. So she had taken a laborious route of the tarmac road, behind hedges and barns, approaching the Sheriff's cottage from behind and waiting in the shelter of an open shed until she had seen Tom Wilson leave and head back towards the village centre. Then she shuffled painfully up the overgrown garden for a chat with John Thurlow.

PARBOLD: KAREN JANE

Born Norwich. Age: 11.6
Height 4ft. 8 ins. Weight 6st. 5lb.
IQ 138 (Blouet Tests)

Hobbies: Reading, nature-study, listening to pop music, social aspects of chapel life. Played part of Angel in nativity play (Infants). Walking-on part, Years II and III. Innkeeper's wife, Year IV. Not an outstanding actress, but can be relied on to do her best—and to remember a big part. Played Margaret in *Fausta*.

Attends every School Camp and all outings. Never wins races, but always enters for them. Will undoubtedly be selected for High School, but would do even better if she were not so withdrawn. She often *appears* not to be doing herself justice, because she is so reticent about her achievements. Firm regime at home—parents will do anything at any time for School or PTA (father an accountant).

Note by Gwynneth Ellis, Class Teacher
I cannot say that I understand this child. Just now and then I believe that I have broken through and made rapport with her, only to find that she has become her introspective self again overnight. Over-strict, not very imaginative nonconformist parents appear to have forced her into a self-sufficiency that is not really self-sufficiency at all.

Sergeant Parrott called on the Parbolds, determined that this time she was going to have her way about the diary, whatever unpleasantness she had to grit her teeth through, whatever complaints were threatened about harassing a child.

Mrs. Parbold was in difficult mood when she came to her door. Sergeant Parrott knew that before they had exchanged more than a couple of sentences. Jane Parbold was not the nervous creature that WPC Price had described—or, at least, she was temporarily on top in the battle with her nerves. She was nervous in a different way. She was taut, but it was a tautness held in check now by a new kind of confidence. WPC Price had said that Mrs. Parbold left all the talking to her husband. Her heart might perhaps be on its way to her mouth now, her insides might be a jumble of worms, but she was fighting back—and winning.

"Mrs. Parbold, I really must insist on a little talk with Karen. I doubt whether it will need to take more than five minutes, and of course it will be in your presence—"

Mrs. Parbold managed to look highly self-satisfied as she stood in the doorway.

"I'm afraid that won't be possible, Officer."

"Mrs. Parbold, I must appeal to you. I know these things are unpleasant for everybody, but the sooner we can tidy them up, the sooner we can all start trying to forget them. Even the tiniest detail might help."

"There's nothing here that can help you."

It was clear from Mrs. Parbold's stance that she did not intend to allow the sergeant over the threshold. Sergeant Parrott toyed with the idea of making a *fait accompli* entry. Surely if she did, she would be able to talk her way out of subsequent trouble. Surely Kenworthy would back her. What did the manual have to say about situations like this? Nothing helpful that she could remember. Non-cooperation like this might be construed as obstruction—but that decision was distinctly senior officers' territory. There were senior officers within easy reach, and no excuse for not consulting them.

"I must ask you to think again, Mrs. Parbold."

"By all means ask me to think. But I'm afraid all the thinking is done. Any more of it is going to be a waste of time."

"You don't want to help, Mrs. Parbold?"

"To help my own flesh and blood. My husband has taken Karen away to stay with relatives. They left a couple of hours ago."

"Then may I ask where—?"

"You may ask. You will not be told."

Mrs. Parbold gave herself additional support by allowing her voice and temper to rise.

"You can take me away and lock me up, if you like. I am digging my heels in. I am making a stand that the country will hear of. I am not going to tell you or anyone else where my child is. I am not going to allow her to be dragged through the apprehension, the misery and the trauma of being grilled by people like you about things that she is not old enough to understand."

"I would have thought you were beyond surprise by now, Mrs. Parbold, at what these children do understand."

"Perhaps I should have used a different word. They may be taught biological facts, but at their age they cannot expect to grasp mature human relationships. My mind is made up. I do not know quite which law you can claim I am breaking, but whatever it is, I shall not be deterred by the consequences."

"I see."

Sergeant Parrott knew that this had to be one for Kenworthy. One saw women like Mrs. Parbold all too often on the magazine programmes that followed the TV news. They kept their children away from school because of squabbles over uniform—or doctrinal teaching. They had chained themselves to railings in their time. They were big with dogmas—and the presenters loved them. One short hope remained.

"And her diary, Mrs. Parbold. She has not taken that with her, I assume?"

"Her diary is already in ashes, Officer. It is a document that we are all trying to forget. Those stupid children were simply *playing*. They had no idea what they were playing at or with."

Mrs. Parbold's courage had continued to rise. She superimposed a veneer of impudence on her attitude.

"Will that be all, Officer?"

"All for now," Sergeant Parrott said.

* * *

The ground in which the pumping station stood had become a rabbit warren, after the survival from myxomatosis, but the immediate surrounds were a stinking mess of rubbish, much of it rotting from the damp. Looking at it, one would not have guessed that the District Council made a weekly collection of refuse in St. Botolph's. Nor would one have thought that four bright twelve-year-old girls, who for all their advanced erotic curiosity had been pointed at respectability from the cradle onwards, would voluntarily have spent their time about here. Certainly one would have thought that a single peep round the broken door would have sent them scurrying.

Kenworthy picked his way among the dumped refrigerators, the putrefying mattresses and the accumulation of old shoes and plastic bottles, the discarded French letters and sanitary towels.

Nothing of the mechanism of the engine-house remained, but one could see where the ends of the driving-shafts had been countersunk into slots in the walls. Owls, bats and pigeons had assumed squatters' rights, each adding an unstinting twopennyworth in the full spirit of the place.

There were the remains of a slatted wooden staircase, which had once had a rope as a banister, spiralling up to what had presumably been a platform round the upper parts of the beam-engine. Kenworthy went up first, testing the treads gingerly, making as sure as he could that they would not give way under his weight: very likely the girls had been up here, probably all four of them at once.

The wind that had lashed Hannah Maslin on her way to see Sheriff Thurlow stabbed in through a hole in the outside wall. At first Kenworthy thought he was going to gain nothing from the top of the steps except for an overview of the rubbish. Then he looked down and saw something that he had not been able to see from ground level. Below the central pile of rubbish, between it and the wall, a sort of alcove had been constructed of old bricks, and under the debris an inner den had been constructed, roofed by rubble supported on an old joist. In this space were four backless seats, each about eighteen inches high, made from short lengths of broken timber. One of these was rather higher and more elaborate than the others, even had a cushion of sorts improvised from old sacking. Davina's throne?

On a board leaning against the wall, a stylized geometrical design had been drawn in black paint. It took the form of one diamond set within another. A blob of black circle had been painted at each angle.

Kenworthy made a rough sketch of the design in his notebook: Was this similar to the Pentangle of mediæval magic? He lowered himself into the alcove, where he found one or two little things: a hair clip, one of those with a peg through a small circle of olive-wood, probably a souvenir from a Mediterranean holiday. It was pushed up against the wall by a corner of one of the seats—not Davina's.

There were graffiti on some of the wall-space, but these did not look like girls' work: *Up the Canaries*—Norwich City Football Club—followed by a four-letter consignment of the same team to unnatural practices. The pumping station was open to all comers, and there could not have been a local boy who had not explored it at some time or other. Perhaps this den was headquarters for more than one group.

Kenworthy clambered cautiously over the rubble pile. Not for the first time since he had come to the Fens, he was glad to get back into open space.

The end-of-day conference was mostly the formality of dismissal. Everybody had the dismal feeling of nothing to show for their plodding. No one believed they had made any progress since midday, but no one made public any sense of frustration. Skeleton night staff took over, in case anything came in, which no one believed it would. Tom Wilson said he would be staying late, but did not say what he would be doing. There was a general impression that tomorrow meant a fresh start with rather less hope of getting anywhere.

Most of them had already heard the news of Karen Parbold's departure. When Sergeant Polly Parrott announced it, there was a ripple among those juniors who were hearing it for the first time. Sergeant Parrott had already quietly reported it to Kenworthy—who, perversely, did not seem to regard it as serious.

"What do you think he's got Connie doing?" Detective-Constable Warburton asked the CID office at large. "He's told her to ask all the women if they know who's had it away with Davina Norris. But she mustn't let them know that that's what she's trying to find out."

"Well, there's a problem in theoretical detection for you, young Dicky," Sergeant Harrold said. "Just tell us how you'd set about it."

"If I were Connie, I'd offer my virtue to the village—to see which frustrated male was that way inclined. That would at least narrow it down."

"Take too long," Sergeant Harrold said, with every appearance of speaking seriously. "She'd be in too much demand."

A little after seven o'clock, Connie Kimble came in to see Kenworthy. She was on her best and most uninviting parade-ground behaviour. Her turn-out was immaculate—but she looked very tired. If only she would show a touch of humanity—! Kenworthy did not doubt that she was human. At least, he thought that her inhumanity was only partial. He believed she was educable—if only someone had the time.

"The toughest assignment that anyone has ever given me in my life," she said. "I knew it was going to be difficult. I ought to have known it was impossible."

"It will be impossible, without a stroke of luck," Kenworthy told her. "Strokes of luck do sometimes happen."

"I've talked to women in this village about everything, especially about the waning standards of today's youth. All

I could get from any of them was a tight-lipped agreement with my own opinions."

Because, as Kenworthy had more than half feared, Connie was not the sort of woman who knew how to talk to people—in such a way that they would talk back. She did not know how to put ordinary people at ease. It would perhaps have been better to have set Patsy Price on to this one.

"At least, I can guarantee that I haven't given away what I was trying to get at."

"Which may mean that no one in St. Botolph's suspects what has happened to Davina. Don't worry, Inspector Kimble. If it could have been broken this way, it would have been in the first hour or two. I don't want you to spend any more major time on this. Just keep it in the back of your mind if something suddenly turns up. For tomorrow, I have something more positive for you. The Parbold child—"

"I was wondering what you were going to do about her."

"Two things. Two opposites. There's nothing illegal in their sending her away from the scene of such things as have been happening here. The parents have been unhelpful— and they seem to have enjoyed being unhelpful. It was irresponsible to destroy her diary—but I can understand why they did. They want to protect her from harassment. And I don't propose to let it be seen that I care two hoots whether Karen Parbold is in St. Botolph's or not."

He looked hard at Connie Kimble, hoping to see her finishing his thinking for him.

"But I do want the child found—without letting it be seen that we're all that worried if we don't find her. I want one of us to talk to her—before anyone can try to stop us. That's your target for tomorrow. You can have any resources we can give you."

Connie underwent a moment human enough for her to blow out her cheeks.

"You know how to set tasks, Mr. Kenworthy."

"You're welcome," Kenworthy told her.

✦ 13 ✦

ACTIVITY IN THE Report Centre had slackened off by eight in the evening. A fire was roaring in the iron stove, and one of the constables who had come in for night duty had disappeared into the village for half an hour and come back with a prodigious supply of chopped logs on a handcart. A wind was whistling in across the marshes. Kenworthy was able at last to feel that he was doing proper justice to the diaries.

Had Davina been so confident that no adult would ever read what she had written? Kenworthy again ran over the entries covering the "offences" of Henry Gower. He felt sure he was right about the sense of occasion in Davina's writing—her best script, sustained throughout the entry. Sometimes, on other days, there had been lapses: fatigue, haste, carelessness, even scribble.

Elsie Frost's account was a weak mirroring of Davina's. Now that he could consider it at leisure and isolate the detail, Kenworthy was even more sure that Davina had told Elsie what to write. Elsie had followed Davina's order of events faithfully—though by no means so vividly. If Davina had set this up, then Elsie had been the weak link in her chain. There must have been times when she had despaired of Elsie. Elsie must have endangered the whole operation. Kenworthy could hear Elsie whining, "But I don't know what to put."

Davina's plan would have fallen to disaster, if Elsie were to weaken. Why had Davina made the others write everything down? To script it, to agree their four stories in advance, so that no one would deviate when they came to be questioned. Bad-tempered, Davina would have told Elsie what to put. And here was Elsie's mnemonic, obediently following Davina's schedule, but poorly written, lacking Davina's fire and adjectives.

Kenworthy turned back a page and reminded himself what Davina had written on the eve of the lesson after school:

"Tomorrow!
    I can hardly sleep for thinking about it. Little does Mr. Henry Gower know what lies in store for him tomorrow."

Davina Norris's evil became more horrifying than ever. She was relishing evil in advance. And what had the other diarists to say about their anticipation? Pauline Dean:

"Davina came home with me after school and we listened to my new record of *Duran Duran*. But she said she did not like it much. That, of course, is because it is mine and not hers. Also, she would not stop talking about you-know-what."

And from Elsie:

"The usual stupid sort of evening that we have in this house. Who wants to watch a documentary about a waterworks when *Top of the Pops* is on?"

If she was even thinking about their nasty little scheme, she had not committed anything to paper about it.

Kenworthy flicked back through Davina's pages, trying to find some reference to how the campaign against Henry Gower had started. He did not find it immediately—but something else caught his eye; being side-tracked was one of the dangers of reading at random.

"To do it properly you have to get eight wooden posts, and drive them into the ground in the shape of one diamond inside another. And you have to have a Bible that nobody has ever read, and it has to be bound in the skin of a baby that has died without being baptized, and between the pages you have to have a new key to a church, one that has never been used to open a church door. And just before sunset, in the loneliest spot you can find, you stand with this Bible in your hand in the middle of the space between the posts. And then this horrible thing will come to you."

Kenworthy had never come across diabolism in practice, that idiotic, masochistic and frequently obscene branch of the occult. Even the Established Church had a department to investigate alleged offences. Where had Davina unearthed this Hammer Film formula? And what effect might obsession with this sort of thing have on a child's brain.

"The thing will be so horrible that you can't bear to look at it. But you *must* look at it, and go on looking at it, because if it sees you are afraid of it, it will kill you."

Eight posts—a diamond within a diamond—Kenworthy looked again at the diagram he had copied from the board in the pumping station.

"But if it sees that you are not afraid of it, then it will do anything for you that you want it to. It will be your slave. The proper word for it is a Familiar."

Were there idiots who really did dabble in this dangerous sort of nonsense?

"I don't know whether I believe in it or not. I don't think I do—but I would dearly like to try it and find out."

Any sensitive and imaginative person mad enough to think that this rigmarole was worth going through might end up seeing all sorts of things approaching his double-diamond. But Davina had not been slow to put her finger on the basic weaknesses.

"The trouble is that you need things that it is not all that easy to lay your hands on. I've thought of two or three ways of getting hold of a church key. We could borrow Mr. Sharvill's, and tell him that we want to go in and do a brass rubbing. Then we could make an impression in a bar of soap. I read about that once, in a book. But who could ever get hold of the skin of an unbaptized baby? Still, what matters is what other people will believe. Elsie will be easy, but it is going to be hard work getting it into Pauline's head, and Karen is a law unto herself."

Kenworthy continued to use Davina as a base, referring to the other two whenever it looked as if they might be fruitful.

"Not allowed to wear my yellow jumper to school today. People!
  Mrs. Ellis makes me sick. She let Karen Parbold play the tambourine again today, and I have never played the tambourine in my life."

Presently a bitter domestic theme began to recur.

"Saturday—the worst night in the week. She hates me and he shows off by trying to pet me. Or else it is the other way round."

And some time later, not long after her tenth birthday:

"What I hate more than anything else in the world is when he tries to make out I am his pet. Tonight he was

in one of his adore-my-darling-daughter moods. Yet
half the time he forgets I exist."

It was all there—the recipe for the child that she was
doomed to become. Or, Kenworthy reflected, all the
boosters and fertilizers, all the sauces and condiments, for
reinforcing, making worse, the child that she had been
fashioned into.

There were broken promises.

"Promised faithfully that she would take me to see
Daddy fly off from Norwich Airport this morning, but
when this morning came, she said she could not face
all those heavy lorries on the road. And I know what
it's really all about, because they had a thunderstorm of
a row after they'd gone to bed."

"He said he really would come to the meeting for the
top class parents tonight, but then there was a telephone call and he had to go and see a man at Fakenham
to collect some brochures he was having printed. Well,
all I can say is that the man from Fakenham must have
come to St. Botolph's with his brochures, because my
father's car stood on the Red Lion car park all evening.
Pauline saw it. I sometimes wonder where he is when
he says he's in Bangkok. Living it up in Marbella?"

There were unfulfilled threats.

"It was supposed to be no television after eight o'clock
for the rest of this week. But I bet I'll be back in their
good books (such as they are) in time for the Old Grey
Whistle Test."

"Just because she said my bedroom was untidy, they
said I couldn't go to the Theatre Royal with them to see
Don Williams, but I happen to have noticed that
they've done nothing about a baby-sitter, and in any

case, they've already paid for the tickets. I'll be going."

There were lavish presents for the world to see.

"I wanted a music centre, but they said there was nothing wrong with that old record-player they must have bought when some museum was being cleared out. And what the hell does a person of my age want with a bloody great doll—even if it can wet its nappies? What pleasure am I supposed to get out of wet nappies? And then I had to be sent upstairs to bring it down and show everybody who came into the house—including Pauline and Karen. Perhaps if I start wetting my own bed again, I shall be more highly thought of."

The things she wanted, of course, were the things she had not got.

"Pauline has a rabbit. Karen has two cats and a dog. Even Elsie has a hamster. And I can't have a kitten because of what it might do to the loose covers."

Worst of all, she was a pawn shoved back and forth in her parents' alarums and excursions. If her father sent her up to her room to repent of some crime, it was her mother who would come upstairs with a packet of crisps for her. If her mother turned off the set while she was trying to watch the Saturday afternoon wrestling, it was her father who came and switched it on again.

"She's always saying how much she loves me when he's here. Some of the time, she even behaves as if she did. But oh, my God!—when he's not here—"

The diary was so full of complaints and envenomed criticisms that Kenworthy wondered when he would find a

page on which she showed spontaneous enjoyment of
anything. She shone at school, but there was nothing and no
one at school who shone in her eyes. Mrs. Ellis, her class
teacher, she hated with a hatred that could be triggered off
by the sight of her coat in the playground or the sound of her
voice in the distance. And the reason for that was inherent
in the footnotes that Kenworthy had seen in the confidential
school records. Davina knew that Gwynneth Ellis could see
through her.

When she first started school, she had idolized Henry
Gower. Then she discovered that Henry Gower did not
exactly idolize her. He seemed fond of her in a strictly
professional way. He admired her talents, particularly her
imaginative creativity and extraordinary command of language. He foresaw a scintillating career for her. (Davina
quoted him as having said to her mother that she was the
most gifted child he ever expected to encounter in his
career.)

But he was not beyond pushing her back in her place
when she was going out of her way to efface lesser mortals.
He made more than one effort to apply a corrective to her
all-pervading egotism. This was what enraged her more
than anything else.

"Henry Gower is a male chauvinist pig. He ought not
to be allowed to be a teacher. He ought to have his
certificate taken away from him."

(She did not specify in her entry for that day what he had
done to deserve such an extreme measure. But it had clearly
been some salutary effort to deflate her.)

And as for her bosom friends, the inseparable four—she
had a searing contempt for them. Indeed, they seemed to
have a searing contempt for each other. (Except that it was
impossible to know much about Karen Parbold. Kenworthy
was wishing more and more that he had her diary in front of
him.)

"My mother says she will fall into a cow-flop one of these days. I only hope I am there to see it happen."

(Pauline on Davina)

"She is a fat cow, and she is going to ruin the puppet show, just as she ruined the Nativity Play and the Carol Concert."

(Elsie on Pauline)

"It is a pity her mother was not on the pill nine months before she was born."

(Davina on Elsie)

One of the most remarkable things—or perhaps on reflection it was not so remarkable—was how much each of the three knew—or seemed to know—about the family intimacies of the others.

"We talked today about making love and having babies. Pauline says that after last night, she'd not be surprised if there's an addition to the family."

That was Davina, when they were between ten and eleven, more than a year, that is, before the upsurge of restlessness that had finally got out of hand.

"It's all very well. I know about animals and all that. But it seems horrible for people to do it. I think it's disgusting. I'm never going to let it happen to me."

(Elsie)

"I can't wait for it to happen to me."

(Davina)

And Little Miss Echo Pauline Dean had said that she could not wait for it to happen to her, either.

And Karen told them that she knew her parents did it. They did it on Saturdays and Wednesdays. She knew because they always came upstairs at a quarter to eleven, instead of midnight, on those nights. And her father always used to come out of their bedroom again and tiptoe along the landing to listen at her door to make sure she was asleep.

"But I wouldn't do it with just anybody. Just think of doing it with somebody with teeth like Frank Mortimer's, or dried *Readibrek* down his front like Cyril Reynolds.

But if you went to a wife-swapping party, you'd have to do it with whoever there was. They put all their car-keyes in a bag, like playing *Scrabble*, and you have to go to whichever car you draw out."

(Pauline)

Pauline should know, because her mother and father once went to a wife-swapping party.

"I heard my Dad telling my Mum. I kept thinking about what I'd do if I were at a wife-swapping party. What if I drew the key of somebody I couldn't stand?"

The problems that present-day youth has to anticipate—

A few pages later Kenworthy made a major discovery. Davina once went away for a few days' holiday with Karen. They stayed with an uncle and aunt of Karen's who lived on the clifftop at Hunstanton, and who took them there in—three disgusted exclamation marks—a G Registration Cortina. Davina gave no quarter. Her diary was a manual of standards from which she would countenance no shortfall. She was acridly critical of somnolent Hunstanton and the Felmers—of their rococo garden, their choice of library books and their addiction to soap opera.

"You're not allowed to open your mouth while *Crossroads* is on."

Could these be the relatives to whom the Parbolds had sent Karen? Kenworthy knew with one of those now-and-then shafts of certainty that they were. He picked up the phone and dialled Connie Kimble's home number.

"I think, Inspector, that I am in a position to save you a good deal of time."

A few minutes later he came upon the cause for the final and fatal schism between Davina and Henry Gower.

It arose in the period when the puppet play first went into rehearsal. There were dissatisfaction and concern among the Four about Henry Gower's ludicrous ideas on casting. There had been similar comments during the run-up periods of all the school's dramatic productions, though never anything as bitter and enduring as this. The Four had no feeling at all for the educational theorist's point of view that histrionic weaklings had sometimes to be made free of the boards for the sake of their social development. They regarded the plum parts as their rights, and the range of talent in St. Botolph's Fen End being what it was, they generally got them—discounting, of course, Elsie, who was destined for ever to be one of the troops in support.

"It is quite impossible—QUITE IMPOSSIBLE—to have Martin Tucksmore doing Dr. Gunther's part. He cannot even read some of the words, and from his dialect you can smell the manure on his boots. Besides—how can anyone who lives in a Council House know anything at all about how a university professor behaves?"

Kenworthy would have said that it was exceptional for country primary school children to be concerned with social status—though in some parts of the country they grew out of their classlessness before they were far into their adolescence. But this vendetta between the girls and a faction who lived in the box-like semis of School Close had been gathering momentum for some weeks now. It was not clear what had started it—probably the Four could not remember. But two things stood out: the girls were merciless—and, alas, they were sincere. They went as a deputation to Henry Gower to dislodge Martin Tucksworth from his part in *Fausta*. But Henry Gower told them he was as responsible for Martin Tucksworth as he was for Davina Norris. Perhaps he also knew more than they thought about this term's undercurrents in his school, and had decided that the time had come to dam off the disturbance. He told the girls that he was pleased with the progress that Martin Tucksworth was making, and that they might be surprised at what he made of the part in the end.

" 'Mr. Gower—if Martin is Dr. Gunther, the play will not be worth putting on.'

'You must allow me to be the judge of that.'

I am determined that we shall get Martin Tucksworth out of *Fausta*, even if we have to come out on strike."

She tried to canvass support from the rest of the school, getting up a petition to the headmaster to which she had even persuaded some of the infants to append their immature signatures.

Henry Gower decided to put a stop to it.

He did not say any more to them there and then. Perhaps he was a sound enough stage-managing psychologist to know how to tease the last shred out of suspense; or perhaps he just wanted cooling-off time. But the girls were aware that they had set off something of extraordinary gravity.

"The four of us stood in front of his desk and he looked at us. Then he went silent and wished we had not started this."

(Elsie)

"Mr. Gower looked kind of hurt, and I wanted to say
that I was sorry. But somehow I couldn't say anything
at all."

(Pauline)

Even Davina did not report as her normal flowing self.
For a change she was succinct—not even reminding herself
of what had happened.

"He did not really say anything, except that he was
going away to think about it. I expect he will come
round to our point of view by morning."

But Henry Gower did not change his mind. It was his
custom to be about the classrooms as early as half past
eight, chatting informally to knots of children about whatever enthusiasms he or they had going. But today he was
very noticeably absent, and did not appear until the school
was already lined up in the assembly hall for prayers. There
was something scrubbed and pallid about his face as the
children stared up at him, unable to understand why no
number had been put up on the hymn-board this morning.
(Pauline was the only one who had recorded these ingredients of atmosphere. Davina omitted them altogether.)

Henry Gower announced that they would not be singing
a hymn. In the frame of mind that he was in, the last thing
on earth that he wanted to do this morning was sing. They
went quietly through the rest of their usual service. He gave
out one or two plain administrative notices—said something
in a whisper to some tot in the infant line. Then he came
forward to the side of his table and everyone in the room
knew that something unprecedented was going to happen.

But not one of the girls recorded the words that Henry
Gower spoke to the school that morning. They could not
bear to recall them. It was plain that his arrows had not
made clean wounds. The girls were hurt—and incapable of
admitting that what Gower had had to say was fair.

"I wish I never had to go into that building again."

(Elsie)

"Nobody would talk to us in the playground. It's all Davina's fault."

(Pauline)

"Henry Gower is going to regret this."

(Davina)

Rehearsals for *Fausta* went on, but from now on the diarists only made desultory references to them. Gower must have known how to maintain a working relationship with his pupils. Their keenness to shine in drama, though dampened, cannot have been entirely extinguished, otherwise there would have been no play.

But it was at this time that a new and unexpected element entered Davina's life.

• 14 •

DAVINA NORRIS WAS not always explicit. Kenworthy was beginning to know her so well that she did not need to be. There had been no mention of Hannah Maslin in her diary until one day only a few weeks ago.

> "She pounced on me as I was passing her gate. It was quite obvious that she was lying in wait for me. She asked me to come into her garden. She said there was something she wanted me to do for her. I had a peculiar feeling as I followed her in. It was like walking on air—the sort of feeling that you get when you're doing something that you've been told strictly not to. When I went through her gate, I felt as if the rest of the world was being shut off behind me."

Throughout this encounter she was sensitive to the hypnotic effect of both the house and the woman. Any normal child would have found Hannah Maslin revolting. It was clear that this had been Davina's first reaction—that this was how she had felt about Hannah Maslin all her life, seeing her from a distance, talking about her to her friends. But what is horrible can also be magnetic. She wrote that part of her wanted to run away, but that something else held her spellbound.

All that the old woman wanted her to do was to pluck a bowlful of conical seed-pods from some plant that she had growing in one of her borders, and to which she could no longer stoop. When this was done, she invited the child into the house and gave her a slice of bread and jam.

"She cut a terribly thick slice, but it was not the same thickness all through, and she spread the butter on it as if she thought I needed rescuing from a famine. But the jam was marvellous. She had made it herself. It was raspberry. I could have done with a second slice, but thought I had better not ask for one."

The house both horrified and enthralled Davina. She was horrified by the dirt, the darkness and the compound smell of age, decay and stale herbal saps. She also saw that it was a house of treasures—and that the old woman knew exactly where to put her hands on objects of unique fascination.

Hannah Maslin asked her if people said that she was a witch. And when the girl did not answer straight away, she took that as meaning that that was what people did say. Davina appeared to have been circumspect about how she answered.

"I was surprised, what sensible things she said, some of the time. I think she might have been an intelligent woman if she had been educated, though many of her ideas are mad. But it wasn't all gibberish that she talked. Some of the words she used were surprising— you'd wonder where she'd learned them. She asked me if I believed in witches, and the best I could think of was that I'd never met one. And I thought then that that was going to be her excuse to tell me she was one herself, but she suddenly stood up and asked me if I would like some more bread and jam.

She went on talking about witches, and how people had definitely believed in them in her precious *good old days*. It was all the usual stuff, about toads, and white horses, and black cats, and throwing salt over your shoulder. Just ordinary superstitions, really."

She told Davina that when she was a girl, an old man living out at Marshall's Fen had tried out some rigmarole that he had found in some book that had been handed down through this family. It was supposed to call up a spirit monster that would be your faithful servant for the rest of your life, if you had the courage to look it in the eye. She did not know how he had got hold of all the bits and pieces that he needed—and she refused for many days to tell Davina what they were. It took him months to collect them all together, then he took them all out to a deserted corner of the fen and went through all the rituals that the book said he must do. Nobody ever found out what happened, but when he came home that night, his hair had turned white. They had to put them away in a mental asylum, and he never talked anything but nonsense for the rest of his life.

Then Hannah asked Davina if she knew where babies came from. Like everybody else in the village, she had heard all sorts of exaggerations about the way sex and reproduction were taught in schools these days. She wanted to know what sort of things Mr. Gower taught them. She talked about sex for the rest of the time that Davina was there, evidently obsessed by it.

"Not that you could call her well-informed. She has the most weird ideas. She believes that when a man pumps his semen into a woman, hundreds of tiny little arms and legs, eyes, ears, noses and all the other parts of us are swimming about in it. And a woman has just as many tiny eyes, toe-nails, hearts, tonsils, livers and so on dancing about in her womb. So it's just a matter of chance which ones join themselves together. And that is why people say that So-and-So has his mother's hair and his father's eyes. She really does believe all this.

She does not think that children in school ought to be taught anything *below the belt*, as she calls it. And she said that when she married her husband, she did not have the faintest idea what he would do to her on their wedding night. She seems to think that this was a far better way of going on. You found things out in your own way, she said. She'd never heard of anybody who hadn't found out what to do, even if they hadn't got it out of a book. Fancy trying to learn that sort of thing out of a book! And she kept coming back to our actual lessons. Did boys and girls sit together when we had that sort of lesson? Did we talk about our lessons a lot out of school? Didn't the boys want to try out all they'd been learning? And she wanted to know if Mr. Gower ever puts his hands where he shouldn't do."

A couple of days later, Davina went back to see the old woman again and this time she did not go into much detail about what they had talked about.

"She gave me a pile of ancient magazines to look at—donkeys' years old, but quite fascinating, if you make allowances."

After that her visits became regular, almost daily, but she wrote less and less about their conversations.

"Called on HM on my way home from school."

At no point did she record hearing any ideas from Hannah Maslin that she proposed to put into practice.

Kenworthy searched the pages of Elsie Frost and Pauline Dean to see whether they had ever accompanied Davina on these afternoon calls, but there was no reference to any such get-together. It looked at if Hannah Maslin was a discovery that Davina did not want to share—at least for the time being. Only once did Pauline complain that she did not know what Davina was doing with herself these days, the moment school was out. She assumed that she was keeping secret assignations with Stephen Lovell who, she thought, had little to commend him.

* * *

Kenworthy's eyes were smarting and the back of his neck was stiff. He left the diaries open on his table in the Report Centre and opted to exercise his limbs.

It was an uninviting night. The wind cutting across from the Wash made a nonsense of the clothes that he was wearing, seemed to find and penetrate every pore between warp and weft.

It was not difficult to remember that the ground where he was walking had once lain under sea. It had been won back by ingenuity and guts—and held against flood and rogue tides by men who liked to think of themselves as a law and a creed apart from the rest of mankind. The forefathers of Hannah Maslin?

He spotted the lighted windows of the Red Lion, set back opposite the church. Pubs, with their careless banter—and their occasionally even more informative silences—had played a vital part in more than one jigsaw that he had put together in communities proud that they would never give anything away.

He walked as far as the Red Lion, waited patiently for the usual chain reaction to work itself through: the politely subdued greeting, the embarrassed drying up of whatever topic had been under discussion by the experts at his moment of entry. Then would follow the ham-handed jocularities of the extrovert-in-residence—there was always one. And sooner or later, with any luck, someone would let drop an unwitting revelation.

He drank bitter beer that tasted as if the pipes from the cellar had not had much recent attention. Then a man called Arthur, who was smoking a cheroot, claimed that he could hear the rattle of handcuffs in his pocket.

Before Kenworthy could shake him by producing a pair, Sheriff John Thurlow came in, in full regalia: brown leather Stetson-type hat, dummy rounds in his gunbelt, scruffy bandanna and rudimentary *chaparejos*. Curiously, no one made any obvious comment in mock-cowboy vernacular.

Someone bought Thurlow a pint of mild. He made some banal remark about the lateness of the spring.

The man with the cheroot had moved closer to Kenworthy.

"We can all feel safe now—the lawman's in."

"Come to swear in a posse, you think?"

Then the man turned from Kenworthy and shouted across the bar to Thurlow.

"I saw you had distinguished company this afternoon, Sheriff. Thought you might have run her in and set up the ducking-stool."

John Thurlow scowled across the room, a look of pure hatred.

"Who was that, then, Arthur?"

"Hannah Maslin," someone said. "Must be the farthest she's walked for forty years. Taking good care she was, too, that not everybody knew who was going to get the benefit of her company."

Unwitting revelation—

While Kenworthy was in the pub, Patsy Price was at the home of the Lovells. She had chosen the time carefully, had waited until she knew their early evening meal would be out of the way and that Lovell *père* would have gone over to the Red Lion. Patsy Price knew the Lovells. She had had to do with them when questions were being asked in the first phase of the Gower case. She knew the temperament of the Lovell father, an intolerant short-haul lorry-driver whose runs were mostly between nearby market towns and the East Anglian ports. She knew the relationship between Lovell and his wife, a timorous little woman who put all her efforts into keeping the peace. She knew young Simon, a somewhat inward-looking and, she suspected, by no means dull boy who had gone on to the secondary school a couple of years ago. When Lovell was safely out of the house, and she calculated that the table would have been cleared for homework, she knocked on the Lovells' door.

Mrs. Lovell looked scared to see her. She looked scared

all the time, by everything that happened or looked as if it was about to happen.

"It's Simon I want to see."

"What's he been doing? You know there was nothing he could tell you."

"There wasn't then. There is now."

"What about? He's a good boy. He's hardly ever out of the house."

"He has to come and go from school, doesn't he?"

"Straight to the bus and straight off it. If I've told him once, I've told him—"

Simon was thirteen, and wearing trousers that had clearly been bought for him when he had not long been twelve. He looked as if puberty was draining him. He was sitting at their dining table, working on elementary quadratic equations. The television was switched on in the same room: his mother had been watching some saga staged in the Deep South. She went and turned the sound down but not off. The boy looked up, frightened in his own right, and further infected by his mother's nerves.

"This needn't take long, Simon. You've done nothing wrong as far as I know. It's information that I'm after."

"Tell the police lady everything she wants to know."

"You've been seeing quite a bit of Davina Norris, Simon."

His mother drew in her breath with shock.

"Simon—!"

"I haven't."

"Somebody's been telling lies about him, Miss Price."

"Simon, I haven't time to waste. Mr. Gower's been killed."

"Well, he doesn't know anything about that, for God's sake."

"It's possible he knows something that might just fit in."

"How can he know anything about that?"

"He can tell me why Davina Norris has suddenly been taking such an interest in him."

It could not be thinkable that her interest was sexual. Any

designs that Davina had in that direction would surely be beamed on someone more mature than Simon Lovell. Unless, of course, she had had some experiment in mind.

"I don't know what you mean," Simon said.

"How often has Davina gone out of her way to meet you off the school bus? And Karen Parbold with her sometimes?"

Both Patsy and his mother could see that the shot had found its mark.

"Of course, if you'd rather wait until your father comes home, I'm sure he would help us to get it out of you."

"For God's sake, Simon, tell the lady what she wants to know."

"How many times did Davina go out of her way to meet you?" Patsy repeated.

"Two or three times."

"More than that."

"Four or five. I can't remember."

"When was the last time?"

"Two or three weeks ago."

"So she's a friend of yours?"

"No. She isn't."

"I should hope not," his mother said.

"So what was she seeing you about?"

He was not far now from crying.

"Was it something she wanted from you?"

He answered with a film of tears across his eyes.

"It was some stuff from the play that she wanted me to get for her."

"What stuff? What play?"

But he no longer seemed able to order his thoughts.

"Tell Miss Price. What stuff? What play? They did a play at their school, Miss Price. Simon was one of the stagehands. Tell Miss Price the name of the play. I've forgotten it."

"*The Alchemist*."

"Ben Jonson?"

Simon nodded. It seemed a positive pleasure to be able to be in agreement with him about something.

"And Davina was interested?"

"She'd been to see it. They got a party up from St. Botolph's school."

"And?"

"Well, there was all sorts of trick-stuff going on on the stage. Blue flashes. Green flashes. Yellow flashes. Explosions. There were chemicals we mixed together to make smoke."

"You know all about this sort of thing, do you, Simon?"

"Our chemistry master was in charge. I had to look after the stuff, and set it off at all the right times."

"You were the special effects man?"

Again, it was a relief to be able to speak to him kindly.

"One of them," he said.

"So where did Davina come into it?"

"She asked me to get her some of the flash and smoke stuff."

"And did you?"

He nodded miserably.

"Only the smoke. We'd used up all the flash powder on the last night."

"Hadn't they had stuff like that for their own play?"

"She couldn't get any of it. She was in some sort of trouble with Mr. Gower."

"Did she tell you what she wanted it for?"

"I think it was some trick she was going to play on those other girls she goes about with. I think it had something to do with the old pumping station. She made me promise I wouldn't tell the other three anything about it."

"But you said that Karen Parbold came with her."

"Not every time. She definitely told me not to tell any of them."

"And was that all you had to do with her?"

"Honest it was, miss."

"But she did come and meet you several times."

"I didn't want to have anything to do with her. I kept

trying to make out I'd forgotten. Then I told her all the chemicals had been locked away in the poisons cupboard. I thought she'd stop pestering me, but it only seemed to make her worse."

WPC Price left mother and son to sort out their own future relationship.

Kenworthy came out of the Red Lion and decided to take one more turn through the village, irrespective of the elements. He did not know what he hoped to find, but could not rid himself of the feeling that there was something behind the walls of this community that they could yield up to him if they only would.

What he did find was a large house, standing in its own grounds. Its gatepost was dignified by the weathered brass plate of Dr. Harcourt Sibley, and underneath this a more modern plaque announced his surgery hours.

The curtains of one of its bay windows were undrawn, and he saw three men drinking brandy from balloon glasses, one of them Chief Inspector Tom Wilson. The hope of being invited to join in that cosiness was altogether too strong: these three looked good company. And to be sure, Wilson saw him and beckoned. One of the others was already on his way to open the door.

His host was Dr. Sibley, the GP who made his own rules about patients' confidences when he thought they were less important than law and order. The other man was the Reverend Michael Palfrey, the vicar.

"Come in, my friend. We are in the middle of a mediæval disputation on the subject of evil. Now you, as yet another whose bread and butter is the sinfulness of the human race—"

"Before you call me friend," Kenworthy said. "Are you really one of mine? How much longer are you going to debar us from talking to Little Miss Norris?"

"Be my guest," Dr. Sibley said.

"And fine hospitality that's likely to be, as long as you insist on keeping her under deep sedation."

"That won't be for much longer. If you'd seen the state she was in this afternoon because you'd purloined her diary, you'd have put her to sleep. But she's got to wake up sometime, and she's got to learn to stay awake with the knowledge that you've read her innermost thoughts. I have a feeling that the only medicine for her is a clean breast."

"If it will come clean."

"I'll be seeing her in the morning—not before ten, and I hope not much later than half past. After that, barring something unforeseen, I don't doubt I can hand her over to your tender therapy. Unless, of course, she follows Elsie Frost's example, and demands the more specialized talents of the cloth. Our friend here is just on his way home from exorcizing Elsie."

"Failing to," the vicar said. "It's going to take a long time to make her whole of this ancient evil."

"Which brings us to our thesis for tonight. At the moment you looked in at my window, Comrade Kenworthy, I was asking Mike and your colleague whether they really believe in evil, or whether what we call evil is no more than the absence of good."

"Any man who believes that," Palfrey said, "might find his opinions violently changed, were he to study what's been going on in this village in recent weeks."

"You mean the combination of Davina Norris and Hannah Maslin?" Kenworthy asked him.

The GP put on a face of mock terror. The vicar shuddered.

"What combination did you say? I did not know there was a liaison between Davina and Hannah Maslin."

"I assure you that there has been. I'm in the middle of reading Davina's diaries."

"It's a combination that would have any prudent heathen crossing himself, as an insurance policy," the doctor said.

Kenworthy stayed sipping brandy a good two hours longer than might have been deemed wise for a man who still had a deal of work to do before he could think of bed.

When he arrived back at the Report Centre, he found a

strange object waiting for him on his desk beside the diaries. It was a dirty and very misshapen old panama, made in the mould of a huge-brimmed cowboy hat.

"Brought in by a farm labourer an hour ago," the night duty sergeant told him. "Found in a ditch about a quarter of a mile west of Mill Lane. Of course, it could have blown there from any distance. And there's no certainty that it's connected with what we're here for. I suppose the Sheriff must lose a hat now and then in a Fen blow."

Kenworthy examined it.

"West of Mill Lane, it could have blown from where Gower was killed. It isn't exactly in the pink of condition, but the material's not rotten: there are no signs of mildew. It can't have been blowing about wild very long."

Constance Kimble drove to Hunstanton in the unlovely hours that preceded the late March dawn. She did not know how she was going to tackle the Karen Parbold angle. There was a firm rubric in the book about what had to be observed when interrogating anyone under seventeen. But it had an *as far as practicable* clause that could be a merciful let-out. She did not know what powers of persuasion she was going to be able to exert over the child's aunt and uncle—or what hook and claw battles she might have to fight with them: it could, in fact, be easier than having to fight her parents. But come to that, she did not even know, beyond Kenworthy's hunch, that Karen Parbold was going to be here. Kenworthy, on the phone last night, had said that he was certain—and there was a strong streak in Connie Kimble that would like to see him proved wrong.

On the other hand, if Kenworthy was right, she knew there was every hope that it would be she who would be ringing him before the morning was over. Because Connie had a hunch as strong as any of his—the hunch that Karen Parbold, isolated from any other key figure in the scenario, might be fairly easy to corner into telling all she knew.

So Connie had wanted to get to Hunstanton early. She wanted to be available for the first opportunity that pre-

sented itself. Perhaps, if she had to make a direct approach,
the best time to do so would be a few minutes after Uncle
had left for work, when Auntie and niece would be
breakfasting informally and unsuspecting in the kitchen
together. Or perhaps, if her luck were in, Karen, in the false
security of this hide-out, would have been allowed some
wild luxury—like being allowed to take the dog for his early
run on the beach.

White Gables, the Felmers' home, was affluent and
affluently placed, towards the southern, Old Hunstanton,
end of the clifftop. Connie drove slowly past it, could see
very little in the tenuous grey of this most unspectacular of
sunrises: even the whiteness of the gables needed an act of
faith in this dismal light. But she noted that there were lights
on behind both upstairs and downstairs windows. Seven-
thirty—and plenty of life was already awake in the establishment. Connie drove down into the town, U-turned and
came back along the cliff, stopped at the far end, in a spot
that she was reasonably certain was out of sight of White
Gables, turned the car again, got out and sampled the sea
air. Or rather, it was a strong off-shore wind that filled her
lungs. In Hunstanton, the East Coast resort that faces West,
the relentless easterly was blowing from behind her back.

And then no less than three pairs of headlights were
coming at speed up the main road out of town, turning down
here from the road above the lighthouse. The first two were
pandas, their blue roof-lights flashing. The third was a
private vehicle, a Sierra, suggesting that a senior officer was
in the immediate wake of his underlings.

The Sierra slowed up as it passed Connie, the man at the
wheel staring out to study her. He seemed to recognize her,
made a sign with his head that he wanted her to follow.
Then all three cars pulled up outside White Gables. The
front door of the house was open, releasing an additional
flood of light, almost before the first of the uniformed men
from the first car had crossed the pavement to the gate.

Connie too drove down, and parked close up behind the
Sierra. She hurried in to join the group that was congesting

the affluent hallway. There was no need to identify herself. The man who had beckoned her was the local superintendent, who knew her.

The big guns were out because Karen Parbold had disappeared from the premises during the night, taking with her in a small suitcase the few things she had brought with her from St. Botolph's Fen End.

· 15 ·

WHAT WAS IT about this year's entries that made the diaries such melancholy reading? Since last Christmas the girls had crossed some sort of threshold. Kenworthy felt a progressive depression. Was it because of the age they had reached? Did they secretly wonder whether they were going to match up to the adulthood they could feel in their veins? Was it all being made worse because they were on the verge of leaving a comfortable little school where they had learned to manage their lives and, by and large, the people about them? Be all that as it may, the pages of the last few months made grey reading.

None of them had anything respectful to say about their families or homes. It was obvious that much of what they recorded was far from the truth. They were exaggerating, each wanting to prove herself the worst done by. Some of what they wrote must be downright distortion. Kenworthy now doubted, for example, whether Pauline Dean's parents really had indulged in wife-swapping. Maybe she had invented that in order to stay abreast. These children—if you could call them children—were competing to report nastiness to each other, and there seemed no limit to what their imaginations could summon up. Elsie Frost was the only one who did not accuse her parents of extra-marital carryings-on. Her complaints—in effect a repetitive and continuous whine—were all concerned with the pin-pricks inherent in a regime of reasonable upbringing. Her most frequent gripe was about the limitations put on listening to pop music.

"And even when I *am* allowed to have it on, the volume has to be turned down so low I can't hear the words."

There was, of course, no first-hand account of depravity within the Parbold household, but sometimes one of the others referred to it, it being apparently generally agreed that this was a sink of iniquity worthy of a place in a Book of Records. One gained the impression that Mrs. Parbold was a voracious nymphomaniac who worked out crafty ambushes for every milkman, meter-reader and door-to-door canvasser in the eastern counties, while her husband's office, when he had been in work, appeared to have been a private brothel and his business journeys a pilgrimage from one exotic whore to the next. Kenworthy was beginning to feel sympathy for the fit of rage in which he had destroyed his daughter's journals.

Davina was more concerned with what went on about her under the blessings of wedlock—though her father did seem to spend an enormous portion of his time away from home. She had acquired a far-reaching expertise. She knew every nuance of the impact of sex on the household. One had to assume that some at least of her chronicling had a basis in fact and observation. She knew from the look on her father's face when her mother's chances of watching a late-night telly film were slight. She even claimed to be able to tell when her parents had wakened early in the morning, and had had what she termed a "quick, sweaty get-together" before breakfast. Sometimes—especially when she had unforgiven domestic defeats to avenge—she took delight in delaying or interrupting their transports. She knew when to wake and scream in simulated nightmare. She could choose the most delicate moment to creep along the landing and scratch her parents' door with the moan that she was going to be sick.

But it was not all sex. In the run-up period to calling up their familiar, she was concerned with the preparations to the exclusion of almost everything else. She was contemptuous of her friends for their gullibility, yet irritable when one of them had a moment of scepticism. They were not keen to believe that the newly cut key that she showed them was one that she had had made in King's Lynn last Saturday, after borrowing the verger's. Karen Parbold wanted to try it in the church door before she would declare herself convinced, but, as Davina had the presence of mind to point out, once it had opened the lock, it would no longer be valid for its fell purpose.

The Bible bound in the skin of an unbaptized infant was, however, a different matter. She had told them Hannah Maslin's story about the old Fenman whose hair had been turned white by his diabolical experiment: that was what set them experimenting themselves. Years ago, Hannah Maslin had somehow gained possession of that Bible, which Davina persuaded her to lend her. It certainly looked the part. There was even a stink of corruption about the book.

> "You could see they were impressed. Elsie Frost backed away from it. Karen Parbold could find nothing to say at all."

Of the actual ritual Davina had written surprisingly little. Kenworthy decided that there might be two possible explanations. Either something had gone wrong with the stage-management; or, possibly, she had had a bad fight. She was a precociously pragmatic child, but an imagination such as hers must surely be susceptible.

She wrote no more about the carrying out of the formula than that it had taken place. She did not even say where. Kenworthy assumed that it was in or near the old engine-house. She did not record what any of the others had found to say. But her signing-off comment that night might be significant.

> "What difference is this going to make to us? Any? I wonder."

Kenworthy detected a certain flatness in the days that followed, but the next weekend the girls went into committee and Davina told them the time had come to start living up to their new status. But there did not seem to be much spontaneous enthusiasm for a bout of wrong-doing.

"I had to remind them of the power we had now.
'You could have fooled me,' Karen Parbold said.
'Well, how shall we know until we try it out?'"

Davina became angry and accused her friends of being chicken-hearted. At last she got them talking of ways to kick over the traces. Elsie Frost suggested a few school rules that they might break, such as all going into class wearing their Wellingtons, the next wet day.

"What a poor specimen that child is! Breaking school rules isn't *evil*. She doesn't know the difference between evil and ordinary naughtiness."

It was then that Davina outlined her scheme for accusing Henry Gower. What she had not gone on to say in her diary was how she had managed to persuade them.

Kenworthy wondered. They were all four of them still smarting after the exhibition that Gower had made of them. There was still strong feeling against them in the school. Some of the other children were still treating them as outcasts. It did not take much to make them believe that they hated Henry Gower. Davina knew how to work on their emotions. And Kenworthy felt sure that not one of them—not even Davina—foresaw how far things would go.

They must punish Henry Gower. But for Davina, Henry Gower would surely have been able to win the others back by now. But she continued to feed the smouldering hate. Consistent hatred needs singleness of mind. To be effective it needs to be whipped up by a leader. Davina was that leader. She would have used rhetoric, mockery, ridicule, would have appealed to the fear of being odd one out.

Davina had the makings of a certain type of politician. The others followed her blindly. It was not long before they could no longer see their way out of what they had started.

Until Elsie Frost broke—

When Inspector Constance Kimble and WPC Patsy Price carried out their first investigation in St. Botolph's Fen End, Davina held firm, and her friends saw no way of unsaying what she had rehearsed them to say. They told their story so well, and with such a degree of coordination, that they might even have ended up partially believing it themselves.

Eventually the policewoman departed. After a preliminary hearing Henry Gower was remanded on bail. The waiting period began. At no point in her diary did Davina show fear—but she was not satisfied. She went on seeing Hannah Maslin. She gave no clue about the extent to which the old woman acted as catalyst.

"This is the beginning. It is Henry Gower's turn to learn a lesson."

But she was already looking round for something new and bigger. Something more *real* she called it. Hardly a day's entry was not fretful because she had not yet thought of anything.

Then she did.

She could not have got far, the Hunstanton superintendent said. She had practically no money with her, and there was no public transport in the middle of the night.

"Hitch-hiking?" Connie Kimble hazarded.

The superintendent shuddered at the prospect and tried to find some hint as to the time at which she might have left the house. Could the Felmers remember hearing any unusual noises in the night?

No. They had heard nothing. All they could say was that Karen had been morose, sulky. But then, she had plenty to be morose about, hadn't she? It was obvious that the

Felmers were already bitterly regretting the role that Mrs. Felmer's sister had cajoled them into playing.

The superintendent left, anxious to get orders out to his patrols. Connie Kimble stayed at White Gables to see if anything could possibly be gleaned.

"Did Karen say anything to you about what's been going on in St. Botolph's?"

"Nothing whatever. We did not allow her to mention the subject. The idea was that she had come here to forget all that."

"Did she behave like a girl who had something on her conscience?"

"Her conscience? *Her* conscience, Inspector? If there's a conscience to be cleared, I would have thought you'd have known where to look for it."

Did they know something? Or was the woman simply putting two and two together from poorly balanced media reports?

"We keep a lot of things docketed at the back of our minds," Connie said, laboriously noncommittal.

"I would have thought that some things were at the front of your minds."

"We are getting close to talking in riddles, Mrs. Felmer. What precisely are you hinting at?"

Not that Connie did not know, but it paid to keep women like Karen's aunt firmly in the grooves.

"I don't know whether you've had much to do with the girl Davina Norris?"

"Yes. I've had a lot to do with her."

"We had her here to stay once—as a friend of Karen's. Those are four days that my husband and I will never forget."

Connie did not reveal that she knew this.

"She led you a dance?"

"There was no pleasing her. Everything in the house, everything we had on the television, everything we suggested to entertain her was inferior. But it was Karen who was led the dance."

"In what respect?"

"Karen is normally a good girl—I mean, apart from the present troubles, which please God are over. But set her down in Davina's company, and Davina is the only one she wants to impress."

"Can you give me any examples?"

"She was not herself at all while the Norris child was here. She was critical, she answered back, she was bad-mannered at table, sharp-tongued—all to impress that young horror."

Connie Kimble came away soon after that, but not before Mrs. Felmer had launched as an afterthought into a torrent of self-exoneration. They could not blame her because Karen was missing.

Not that Karen was missing for very much longer. She was not making any effort to conceal herself. A squad car picked her up along the main road between Heacham and Snettisham. She looked woebegone, was snuffling and foot-blistered, and was carrying a suitcase that by now she was having to change from hand to hand every few yards.

She said simply that she had decided to go home; weary resignation was all she demonstrated as she climbed into the police car. Connie did not trouble to invent an excuse for going through her suitcase. At the bottom of it there was a fairly new hardbacked exercise book that was in effect the current volume of her diary, begun only a matter of weeks ago—the only part of her life's record that her father had not incinerated, presumably because she had kept it hidden while the fury was on.

Connie had no time to read it properly, but she realized before she had turned many pages that the sooner this was in Kenworthy's hands, the better.

Tom Wilson had had them put up at a small commercial hotel in King's Lynn, but it was well past the end of the working day—almost past the end of the hotel day—before Kenworthy saw his room. Even then he went on working, and was less than in love with the notion of getting up when the time for that arrived. Nevertheless he stirred himself—at the hour when Connie was already on the clifftop at Hunstanton. He was in the middle of shaving when Sergeant Parrott knocked on his door. She gave the impression of having been happily up and about for hours.

"Oh, I'm sorry, sir."

"Come in, Sergeant Parrott. Come in and watch me shave. That always used to be one of the major delights of the Kenworthy homestead, when they were lucky enough to have Daddy home."

She was for backing apologetically away, but he insisted.

"It's only, sir, that I'd like a quick look at the diaries. You've been hogging them."

"They're worth hogging."

"If I could have a quick peep before breakfast—"

"A quick peep could be misleading. Concentrate on the last four months."

"I did my own share of reading last night, sir."

Sergeant Parrott managed to look willowy, fresh and agile even at this hour of the morning. She was going to mature into an elegant woman, but it was not going to be the same kind of elegance as Connie's, which rested squarely on her somewhat heavy taste in plain costume.

"I got hold of a copy of *Fausta*. A very wholesome piece of drama—as one would expect from Henry Gower."

"Relieved to hear it."

"Proving that the Devil is nobody. Anyone with a modicum of single-mindedness can stand up to him."

"Unless they don't want to. Tell me, Sergeant Parrott—do you believe there *is* such a thing as evil? Or is evil merely the absence of good?"

"May I answer that after we've talked to Davina Norris, sir? I take it she's not going to be stockaded from us for ever?"

"Indeed not. I have that well in hand. She should be available from shortly after ten-thirty. Which gives us time to pay another key call first."

"Hannah Maslin?"

"The same. We shall find out a lot about Davina Norris, if we can only sound the right chords in old Hannah."

"There's another woman you ought to talk to too, sir. It was from Mrs. Ellis that I borrowed the script of *Fausta*. She teaches the second class from the top. Gwynneth Ellis. If you remember, she had added a supplementary note to all the school record cards that we've seen."

"Yes, Sergeant Parrott, I do remember. I do have the habit of remembering all sorts of bits and pieces of arcane information, but I expect I shall lose this talent as senility gradually takes hold."

Sergeant Parrott had heard of his bludgeoning sarcasm, but this was the first real example of it she had had. She looked at him uncertainly, but went on talking as if he had not answered her in that vein. There were many things about Kenworthy that she did not yet understand; one of them was that she was not meant to understand him.

"Then you'll also remember that there was always some nuance in which her judgement varied from Henry Gower's."

"Well spotted, Sergeant."

"She added a footnote about Davina's sulkiness. She said it was a pity that Pauline Dean was in a group dominated by one particular personality. And she had a higher opinion of Elsie Frost's intelligence than Gower had. In fact, Gwynneth Ellis's opinions generally do differ from the party line. Pen and paper tend to inhibit the vigour of her views, but in one to one conversation she expresses herself most unambiguously."

"Do you propose to go into more detail?"

"I think you'd better have a word with Mrs. Ellis yourself, sir. I think you'll have fun with her."

Kenworthy looked at her with his razor poised. Lather had dried on his face while she had been talking.

"Sergeant Parrott, you remind me of my daughter when she was six. Henceforth I am going to call you Polly. You can regard that as a special reward."

"A reward, sir? For what?"

"For remembering something that some of my sergeants forget: that the reason the Yard sends Inspectors and Chief Inspectors out into the deep field is mainly to keep them amused. So that they can have fun. I take it you have more valid reasons for playing cat and mouse with me about Mrs. Ellis? You have taken a liking to St. Botolph's Fen End and would like to prolong our stay there, perhaps?"

"No, sir. It's just that I may be wrong about her. And I have a feeling that you will be sure—at once."

"Still a little scared of me, aren't you, Polly?"

"Yes and no, sir."

"On the whole not a bad thing to be," Kenworthy said. "It's better to be on the safe side. What did Mrs. Ellis say that particularly struck you?"

"That Davina Norris isn't the real leader of the little group. She's the liveliest. When they're playing pranks, she's the chief executive, Mrs. Ellis says."

"But the prime mover—?"

"Is the one who doesn't talk much. Karen Parbold. She moulds the shot for Davina to fire. Pauline Dean falls in line to impress. Elsie Frost just doesn't seem to be able to help tagging along."

• 16 •

KENWORTHY PICKED UP the tattered old straw sombrero that had blown westwards across Mill Lane and carried it in his hand down to Hannah Maslin's.

"What on earth?" Sergeant Parrott asked him.

"This may possibly be, Sergeant Parrott, the hat worn by the man who killed Henry Gower, while he was on his way to do the foul deed. If not, we have to eliminate it. I'm sorry—am I anticipating? I don't want to spoil your fun."

"Are you never going to let me forget I said that?"

"Don't take it to heart, Polly. I'm always like this when a case reaches this stage. When you've been in a strange town, have you never driven three times past your destination, in full sight of it, along one-way streets that you see no escape from—because there's no way to get across to where you want to be?"

"I know the feeling."

"I think I'm getting an idea of what happened. But I still don't know how I'm going to get through to it. And when I'm in this frame of mind, there is always the thought that perhaps I never will."

Kenworthy held the gate open for Sergeant Parrott. At the top end of Hannah Maslin's garden, a child under school age was beginning to become fractious in a pushchair parked beside the back door. Kenworthy knocked and opened the door in the same second. Hannah Maslin scowled at him. She was showing Linda Calvert something at the bottom of a tin tea-caddy.

"You can see how much there is left."

"There's not enough there to brew a couple of pots."

"This is all I've got. I can't get about like I used to. I told you when you came before—when it's done, it's done."

"It did me so much good. It's the only thing that ever has done me any good."

"You can have what there is, and welcome. I always said the day would come when I'd have to give up."

"Well, can you tell me what the ingredients are? Tell me where to go to find them for myself. Then I could bring them to you, and you could make them up for me."

"It's the wrong time of year."

Was there a hint of triumph in the old woman's tone? As if she had proved the helplessness of a world that could no longer turn to her?

"It isn't in seed till the autumn. Then you've got to wait for them to dry out."

"Well, will you tell me the names of the herbs you need? Then perhaps—"

"And give you my secrets?"

Mrs. Maslin put the tea-caddy away and closed her cupboard door.

"I wouldn't be going into competition with you," the young woman said. "If you'll tell me the names of the plants you need, I'll go round collecting them for you. I'll make a hobby of it. Then you can stay in business."

Kenworthy put down the straw Stetson prominently on the corner of the table. Hannah Maslin looked at it and scowled again. She also half-turned and produced a special personal scowl for Sergeant Parrott's benefit. Outside on the garden path the child began to cry. The young woman wished the old one goodbye, but her only response was a tightening of her lips.

"You missed a chance there," Kenworthy said, when the door had closed behind Linda Calvert. "That offer was made in perfect good will. It could have led to a useful partnership."

Hannah Maslin said nothing.

"But I'm forgetting, Mrs. Maslin. Partnership is not your strong line, is it? It's either lone or nothing, with you, isn't it?"

She received this in aggressive silence. Kenworthy picked up the hat and twirled it round with his forefinger under the crown.

"We both know when you last saw this, don't we? Yesterday your lips were sealed. You wouldn't say a word. You wouldn't implicate Sheriff John Thurlow, because you weren't certain it was him that you'd seen, going down Mill Lane behind Davina Norris and the teacher. What was it that made you suspicious?"

She was trying to stare him out.

"All right—if you won't tell me, I'll tell you, shall I? In outline, in silhouette, in the dusk, it looked like the Sheriff. But the man's gait was wrong, the way he walked, the way he held his shoulders. So you went to see the Sheriff yesterday afternoon. You braved the fen blast. You hoped no one had seen you. And you established to your satisfaction that he hadn't been down this way, the night before last."

She was taking good care not to look impressed by his reasoning. Not by any slip of her features did she intend to betray that he was right.

"Whose hat is this one, Mrs. Maslin?"

"It isn't John Thurlow's. He wears better ones than that."

"I find all this wholly admirable," Kenworthy said. "You have a splendid regard for fairness and truth. If every witness I have to deal with in my job was as scrupulous as you are, there'd be a lot less time wasted—and perhaps less injustices done. Wholly admirable—and what a contrast to what you have to answer for about Davina Norris."

"I have nothing to answer for about Davina Norris."

"No? You filled her mind with enough filth and rottenness, didn't you?"

"There was no room in her mind for any more filth and nastiness than were in it already."

"Do you know, Mrs. Maslin, that every time she left

here, she went home and wrote down every word you had said to her?"

It looked as if she was going to return to her truculent silence.

"Doesn't that worry you, Mrs. Maslin," Sergeant Parrott unexpectedly asked her, "that the things you said meant so much to her?"

"Why should it worry me? All I did was answer the questions she asked me."

"Yes—and what sort of questions were they?" Kenworthy put in. "Witchcraft. Devilcraft. Calling up evil spirits. You even lent her that obscene Bible that was supposed to be bound in a baby's skin."

"She was interested."

"And if she'd been interested in putting poison into her mother's gin bottle, what jalop would you have given her?"

"That's a wild and wicked thing to say, Mr. Kenworthy. The word poison was never mentioned between us. I've never had to do with poisons in my life: only to help people get over them. I put no badness into Davina. The badness was all there already."

"And you had the time of your life exploring that badness, encouraging it."

Sergeant Parrott broke in again. "You've found out it wasn't John Thurlow who followed her down the lane. Who do you think it was now?"

"What sort of a future do you think Davina Norris has?" Kenworthy asked.

"You must at least have asked yourself who it might have been. You must have narrowed it down," Sergeant Parrott said.

"Did you know that she was already looking for a man she could go the whole hog with?" Kenworthy flung at her.

Alternating, giving her no time to answer, even if she would have done, the pair of them bombarded her with questions. Kenworthy had moved across the room so that his voice was stabbing the opposite ear from Sergeant Parrott's target.

"What did you tell her when she asked you what it was like, going the whole hog with a man?"

"You must have narrowed it down. You must have ended up with a list of not more than two or three."

"Did she ask you what it was like, going with a man?"

"Who are you going to call on this afternoon? Who's the next one you want to check up on, who might have come down the road wearing this hat?"

"Did you warn her about venereal diseases?"

Then suddenly they stopped. The silence hit the squalid little living-room as if the echoes of the last question could be heard dying away into it.

Then Kenworthy repeated his last question.

"Did you warn her about venereal diseases?"

"I don't know anything about any men she was going with."

"I asked you who you are proposing to call on this afternoon, Mrs. Maslin," Sergeant Parrott said.

"Oh, don't start all that again. I can't stand it."

She was looking at them wildly. Kenworthy began to speak in quiet contrast to the frenzy they had been hurling at her.

"We have a lot of questions to which we need your answers, Mrs. Maslin. If you don't want to answer them here, I shall have to ask you to accompany us to King's Lynn police station."

Even the stilted formality of a word like *accompany* helped to ram it home to her that Kenworthy was in earnest. If they took her away from her home, there was no telling how long it would be before she saw it again. Her fear was now showing through.

"Don't start shouting again at me from both sides. I can't stand that. I'll tell you as much as I can."

"That's better."

"But it won't be much, because I don't know much. I haven't the slightest idea who it was went down Mill Lane—now that I know it wasn't John Thurlow. Somebody wanted to look like him, and that was a dirty trick. They can laugh at John Thurlow—those who don't know what he's done for his mother—"

"And you admire him for that? Excellent! That's twice you've come out with truly admirable thoughts, Mrs. Maslin. But I don't see how it squares up with your sessions with Davina."

"I did Davina no harm. There was no harm anyone could do her—as you'd find out for yourself, if you bothered to go into it properly. Oh, she's bad. But aren't all of us bad? Doesn't it say so in the Bible and the prayer-book? There is no health in us? But I've never known anyone as bad as Davina. There's something about her that was—oh, I don't know how to put it—"

"I think *fascinating* is the word you are looking for," Kenworthy said. "Yes. I can see you were fascinated. I can see why you let her have her head when she came here to talk. It was encouraging her to play with that obscene Bible that was irresponsible—among other things."

"How could I stop her?"

"You should never have told her that story about it."

"She could have heard it from any of the old ones in the village."

"So you wanted to know if it would work if she tried it?"

"It didn't do them any harm, did it?"

"How can you possibly say such a thing? I suppose you think they didn't do Henry Gower any harm, either? And don't forget that those other girls haven't Davina's strength of character. She *has* strength of character, even if a lot of it does go the wrong way."

"I don't know the other girls. I'm not interested in them."

"But you were fascinated by Davina."

"Because I was sorry for her. Do you know what sort of life she leads? I've always thought that mine was lousy enough. Mine was dirty. I knew what it was to go hungry. I'd a leather strap across my backside when I was three years old, and four years old—and fifteen. I've known my father come home drunk to find my mother even drunker on the scullery floor after downing a couple of bottles of her homemade parsnip wine. The Norrises get through as much money in a month as my parents saw in ten years. And what does it do for them? Saddles them with misery."

Hannah Maslin was beginning to wheeze from the emotional effort she was putting into her words.

"You know that the girl's father's a criminal, don't you—a real criminal? The sort of criminal that you people don't get on to because you know in advance he's too clever for you. Do you know what it's like for a girl growing up to know that? Because Davina Norris does know it. She's known it since she was a tot, from the things her ears have picked up. Do you know why that marriage was not broken up years ago? Because of the way the money's tied up. Because everything he's swindled from people is put down in his wife's name, where it's safe from the bailiffs. That's the only reason he comes home to her. And she's there when he does come home, because all she has to live on is what he gives her. That's what Davina Norris is stuck in the middle of."

There was a new hideousness in Hannah Maslin's face, as if the effort to convince them was draining every reserve of will-power she could muster.

"Do you know that neither of them wants her, or ever did want her? Do you know what it's like to be told that? I do, because I was reminded often enough of the same thing. And then to be used, the way they have used her. They each use her to punish the other with. When they're not speaking to each other she's the one who has to pass messages between them."

"And you think all this gives a child an excuse to be bad for the sake of being bad?"

"It doesn't make for goodness, that's for sure."

"This girl has a good brain."

"And since when has a brain been a comfort to anyone? Nine times out of ten, people with brains end up in the worst trouble."

That was Hannah Maslin's firm belief. There was no

point in trying to argue against it. Brains were a self-deluding peril.

"Do you know how much her mother drinks? Do you know what time in the day she starts drinking? Do you know that the only peace the child has in the evening is after her mother has passed out? Do you know what a woman's like before she's had her first drink of the day? Or when she's had too much but still not enough? Is there any wonder that the child goes ranging round the lanes at night, when she ought to be sitting in comfort at home?"

"From something she wrote in her diary," Kenworthy said, "she was planning to do what she called something *real*—and by that she meant something really bad, some-thing shockingly bad—something she was hoping would happen in the next month or so. Did she say anything about that to you?"

"She did not."

"We think it had something to do with going with a man. Did you gather that there was a particular man who interested her?"

"No. But I remember saying to myself: Here's a young lady who's going to have a prick inside her before she's much older."

"What made you think that?"

"She thought too much about it. She wanted to know too much about it. It was on her mind all the time. And to my way of thinking, all those lessons at school only encouraged her."

"So did you."

"It's not fair to say that. I used to let her run on. It was—Mr. Kenworthy said the word—it was fascinating."

"So let's say, for the sake of argument, she had decided to go with a man. It had to be someone who was available—that means someone in St. Botolph's Fen End, or someone who comes here pretty often. Now who would that be likely to be?"

"How can I tell?"

"How many patients have you, Mrs. Maslin?"

She was momentarily put out by the change of subject. It was a favourite device of Kenworthy's.

"Oh, all that's fallen off," she said. "Sometimes I go three or four weeks, and nobody comes."

"On the whole, I suppose, you see more women than men. Women talk a lot, don't they? What do the other women in this village think of Davina Norris?"

"They all think she's bad."

"I've got a feeling, Mrs. Maslin, that you could get to the bottom of this business before we do. People talk to you, don't they—not everybody, perhaps—but there are people who trust you. You'll find out who it was who went down Mill Lane after Henry Gower and the girl. And when you do, we shall expect you to tell us."

"That will depend."

"No. It will not depend. It won't depend on anything. We want it cleared up before the wrong man is blamed for it. As John Thurlow might have been blamed."

"An interesting phenomenon," Kenworthy said, as they were walking back up the village street. "The old girl hates nearly everybody. In the normal way, she isn't even sorry for people in trouble—unless they come and ask her to do something for them. A young woman with asthma gets all her attention—till she runs out of medicine. A young copper with boils on his bum gets preferential treatment. She knows those things are within her capacity. So she sheds everything else and becomes a different woman. She'll find out who killed Henry Gower. And she'll try to stand out from telling us. Of course, I shall have her watched. I'll have Tom Wilson put his DCs on her round the clock to see if she goes anywhere, if anyone comes to see her, who she talks to. Then if we can find where she gets information from, we can go to the same source ourselves. Hey-ho, Davina—here we come."

· 17 ·

"THE DOG THAT didn't bark," Kenworthy said, slackening their steps when they came in sight of the Norrises' home.

"Something doesn't fit?" Polly Parrott asked.

"I'm just thinking about the things that Davina missed out of her diary: her father's crimes, passing messages when her parents were not on speaking terms, being told she wasn't wanted. Her mother's drunken bouts—and perhaps even worse, her sober ones. Yet these things were always on top of her mind. She talked to Hannah Maslin about them—but she wouldn't put them on paper. So what does that tell us?"

"Ask me again when we've talked to her," Polly said.

They walked up the drive. The two-car garage door stood open and they saw the boot of a blue Citroën Diane, current year's registration. Cynthia Norris stood in her front window, dressed not to kill, but to impress them with her respectability. Sergeant Parrott told Kenworthy afterwards that even her make-up had been contrived to conceal recent harassment. She hurried to open the door to them, smiling at them with a well-considered undertone of sadness. There was enough light in her eyes to suggest that she had got herself topped up to precisely the right level.

"How's the patient this morning?" Kenworthy asked.

"Oh, so much better. You could almost call her her normal, natural self. I wish I had the resilience of the young."

"We *shall* have to talk to her, Mrs. Norris."

"What else are you here for? If I might just have a word, Mr. Kenworthy: I owe one of your colleagues an apology. I know I was very rude and uncooperative with that young policewoman."

"I think you'll find WPC Price forgiving. It's not to be wondered at if you lost your control. You've had a lot to stand up to."

"If only my husband were here—"

"What will he have to say about all this when he knows?"

"He'll see everything straight away in its proper perspective. He's like that. If only he didn't have to go away so much—But a man has to work for a living, with two demanding females like Davina and me to cater for."

"Where's Davina at this moment? Still in bed?"

"No. She got up as soon as the doctor had seen her. She said she was going to square her room up, then get on with some sewing."

"Perhaps we could talk to her up there?"

"It's as good a place as any. Am I allowed to hear what you say to her?"

"It would be professionally wrong to try to stop you—as well as ham-fisted."

The girl's bedsit—that was what it amounted to—was airy, tidy, and a hive of activity. Davina had got out a cardboard box and was sorting out scraps of material cut to an octagonal template. They looked as if they were destined for a patchwork quilt.

"What are you making?" Kenworthy asked her, in the tone of royalty visiting a Christmas ward.

"Oh, it's only a cover for my doll's pram. Mummy's always telling me I'm too old for dolls, and I suppose they do bore me really. But I love making things. The best of making them doll-size, is you do have some hope of finishing them."

"Show the gentlemen the pillow-slip you embroidered last year," her mother told her.

They duly admired it. This was without doubt a scenario rapidly scripted by mother and daughter. Kenworthy let it take its course. He believed in allowing people to work through their pretences—if there was time. They usually peeled layer after layer away from themselves.

"You didn't say anything in your diary about needle-work," he said, not unsweetly, but letting her see that it was business they were here to talk about.

Davina bit her lower lip and dropped her eyes.

"Oh, my diary! You must have been shocked by my diary."

"It's a very unusual one," he said.

"You didn't take it all seriously, I hope?"

"I take everything seriously."

"Yes, but—"

She tried a little laugh—not very successfully. "My diary was not meant for anyone but me to read, you know."

"I hope not."

"Nearly everything in it happened only in my imagination."

She waited for Kenworthy's reaction, and he did not oblige her.

"I mean, surely, Chief Inspector . . . You don't think—?"

"What do you expect me to think?"

"I'm afraid I sometimes let my imagination run away with me, Mr. Kenworthy."

"So let's just mention one or two of the things that you wrote about, shall we? The shameful morals of Karen Parbold's mother and father—"

Davina laughed.

"That was just a big joke—because nothing could be further from the truth. They're so stuffy, those two—and nobody knows that better than Karen."

"Pauline Dean's parents at a wife-swapping party."

Mrs. Norris gasped.

"Pauline made that up herself," Davina said, "to make herself look big."

"I won't call your imagination rich. Let's say it's hyper-active."

"I've never read these diaries," her mother interrupted. "But from what Davina's been telling me, there's some pretty scurrilous stuff in them."

"I never meant to hurt anyone," Davina said.

"You meant to hurt Mr. Gower. You said so in so many words."

If Davina had been a child film actress, there would have been no need for glycerine tears. There was a real one swelling into the corner of her eye now.

"It was wicked and unforgivable, and I don't ever expect to be forgiven. We wanted to get even with him because he showed us up in school assembly. I know that's no excuse. But we wouldn't have gone through with it, you know—not all the way. We meant to tell the truth just before the court."

That was of course a lie, monstrous and monstrously impudent. Kenworthy appeared to accept it, even though he might have pointed out that there was no such indication in the diary. He went on as gently as he had been talking all the time:

"And all that ugly nonsense you talked with Mrs. Maslin? That was all a figment of your imagination too?"

"When you're with Mrs. Maslin, you can't help talking about things like that."

"To be talking to Mrs. Maslin at all—in that slum—!" her mother said.

"Mummy, Mrs. Maslin isn't *bad*. She can't help her appearance, can she?"

"She can help the things she talks to eleven-year-olds about."

"Some of us are twelve, Mummy."

"Let's move on, shall we?" Kenworthy said. "Let's not forget our reason for being here. Someone killed Mr. Gower."

"I know. I still can't believe it."

"If he hadn't seen you going down Mill Lane on a dark night, Davina, Mr. Gower wouldn't have gone down there after you."

Davina looked very gravely concerned.

"And, you know, someone else followed him."

"That silly man who goes about wearing a six-shooter."

"In point of fact it wasn't. Now will you tell me why you were out of doors at all on such an inhospitable night?"

"I just wanted to think."

"You spend a lot of your time thinking, don't you?"

"This wasn't ordinary."

She looked in appeal at her mother. "Mummy—do we have to talk about this?"

"I'm afraid we do, darling."

"You had something on your mind that wasn't at all ordinary, Davina."

Davina was now finally weeping. Kenworthy was uninfluenced.

"So let's not dodge the crux of the matter. The doctors can tell what you've been up to."

"They can't. They can't, they can't, they can't! They've got it all wrong."

"Mrs. Norris—she went with a man. It's of prime importance that we find out who that man was."

"I have never been with any man."

"You have. The evidence is undeniable. You said in your diary that you were going to."

"I did not. You cannot show me anywhere in my diary where I said that, Mr. Kenworthy."

"Perhaps not in those words. You said you were going to do something *real*, in the near future. The doctors can tell when you've done something real."

But that was the moment at which a telephone chose to ring on an extension in another bedroom. Mrs. Norris looked at Kenworthy, and he nodded to her to go and take the call. Kenworthy signalled to Polly.

"Do your stuff, Sergeant Parrott."

And in the next five minutes, no one would have guessed that Sergeant Parrott normally spoke with an upper-crust accent. She laid aside as if they did not exist any pretensions to serenity and elegance. This was the Polly Parrott more at home picking up junkies in public lavatories.

"You ballast-brained little bitch—what do you take us for?"

Davina recognized at once the Greek-meets-Greek syndrome. From bouncing confidence she had retreated into self-pity. But what she was registering now was the beginning of terror—and this was not acting.

"Have you given any thought to what's going to happen to you, you vile little brat?"

"They can't send me to prison."

"They can do the next best thing. I never saw anyone in my life sailing as close to a care and protection order as you are."

But even now that she had to recognize her cause was lost, Davina was not beyond a surly rejoinder.

"I don't know what you mean."

"If ever I saw a child in need of protection from moral danger—"

Sergeant Parrott threw out a hand to indicate the wall-friezes, the posters, the colourful coverlet, the books and the LPs. "You've done nothing but complain of your surroundings all your life. But by God, you're going to miss them if you have to spend the next six years of your life in an institution. I can think of some foster-parents I'd dearly like to see you answerable to."

This time Davina made no rejoinder.

"You know things that we need to know, Davina. I don't have to spell them out for you. Cooperation is your only chance—and I wouldn't set even that too high. Write it down for us, if you find it too embarrassing to talk about. We'll give you till tea-time."

Kenworthy had one other piece of business to do. He brought out of his pocket an olive-wood hairslide.

"Yours?"

Surprise—

"Yes. Mummy bought it for me in the market at Fuengirola. Where did you find it?"

"In the pumphouse. It had fallen down by one of the seats."

She held out her hand for it.

"I'm going to hang on to it for the time being. Sergeant Parrott will give you a receipt. I'm rather surprised, Davina. I would have expected to find it by one of the other seats."

She looked at him without any idea what he was getting at.

"There was one seat that struck me as more like a throne. I would have thought that was where you sat for your devil-worship."

"Oh, no. That was always Karen's place."

"I asked you a question as we were going in, Sergeant Parrott."

"About the things she didn't refer to in her diary."

"Her father's way of earning a living, her mother's drink: some of the things she'd talked to Hannah Maslin about, but didn't put down in black and white."

"Because those are the things that she's failing to face up to. Those are the things she'd like to hide from if she could."

"Well done, Polly. And well done in there, by the way."

"If it works—"

"It will work. That and a few other things."

◆ 18 ◆

"If you don't mind my saying so," Connie said, "this is something you'll want to look at immediately."

The village hall looked more like a social centre. Tom Wilson and his DCs were in committee. A uniform sergeant was expansively on the phone to his parent station. WPC Price was talking to a St. Botolph's housewife at a table in a corner.

So again he had to find somewhere where he could do uninterrupted justice to a diary. He went again to Mrs. Jeffs's cottage. And the down-to-earth London-born housewife was delighted to see him. Her hair was out of kerchief and curlers, which suggested that she had been hoping for another visit. The upturned bicycle had been removed from the hearth-rug—which seemed to rob the room of more than half its character.

Kenworthy went straight to the key dates. Karen Parbold's account of the alleged out-of-class lesson in human biology contained precisely the same details as Davina's, and some of the sentences were identical. Even more interesting was a folded sheet of paper between the pages, which contained brief pencilled notes of the structure of these paragraphs.

Stock-room. Drops catch
Description. Blue end.
Gets bigger, throbbing.
We touch. (Elsie wouldn't). He flinches. Touches D.
Felt how hard.

For a moment the detail was so vivid that Kenworthy had
the horrified feeling that the incident had happened after all.
But it hadn't, and these preliminary notes were in Karen
Parbold's handwriting. It looked as if it was she who had
collated the bones of the narrative, perhaps after consulta-
tion with Davina or the whole group. Karen had been
excited, the day Davina had come back from Hannah
Maslin's with the skin-bound Bible story.

> "This is marvellous! A silly tale, but we could have a
> lot of fun out of it. Some people will believe any-
> thing."

The account of their attempt to call up a familiar made it
clear why Davina had been notably uninformative about the
event.

> "D ruined the whole thing. To make the smoke she had
> to have liquids in two separate bottles, and let them run
> together. But she tripped over a stone and smashed
> both bottles before we started. We were all nearly
> choked. My eyes were still smarting at bedtime. And
> that moron in a cowboy hat was watching from the
> sea-wall.
>   No vile monster. No slave for life. I never believed
> this rubbish anyway, and I don't think D did, though
> she wanted to. But it was a joy to see how scared stiff
> Elsie and Pauline were."

Karen's diary was the least even of the four. She did not
always manage daily entries, and sometimes would produce
nothing for a whole week. Sometimes her entries were in
note-form, as at bedtime on the night of the murder.

> "Huge excitement. HG hanging about after school.
> Scared Elsie Frost, went off talking to Davina. Scan-
> dal. Telephones gone mad all over St. B. Solicitors are
> going to have HG arrested. Yippee! Middle evening,

our phone rang—HG himself. Nerve! Wouldn't have rung my father if he'd heard what he's been saying about him."

Maisie Jeffs came in with coffee: Camp again.

"What? Another load of homework?"

"Just a short one this time. How well do you know the Parbolds, Maisie?"

"Not my cup of tea, and I'm not theirs. They're chapel."

"And you're church?"

"No, I'm nothing. They're strict. The Devil lives in a bottle and Jesus Christ came down on earth to stop people doing football pools. But it isn't that. They don't mix. This is a queer village. There are the locals, and they'll pass the time with anybody, though you can never get past a certain point with them. Then there are people like us, who've come here for the work. Then there are people like the Norrises and Parbolds. They think they're some sort of chosen tribe."

Maisie Jeffs lit herself a cigarette and went on talking with it loosely between her lips.

"Take the Parent-Teachers. When the Norrises and that lot moved in, they took it over. Nobody else could get a word in edgeways. Oh, they've done good work. But these things lead to favouritism, don't they? And when the headmaster is in and out of their homes—"

"All their homes?"

"Some more than others. He was in and out of the Parbolds' three or four times a week. Thick as thieves, they were. But of course that all stopped when the police had to be called in."

Kenworthy delegated Karen Parbold to Sergeant Parrott, with Patsy Price to take notes. He told Connie it wasn't a job for her because she'd talked to the child in the car, and he did not want to sit in on the confrontation himself because he did not want to inhibit Polly's style.

But it was impossible not to be inhibited by the inevitable

presence of Mrs. Parbold. Sergeant Parrott knew that
sooner or later it would pay off to swing into fishwife tone
and tactics, but first she used reason and a hint that
forgiveness could be earned by cooperation now.

None of this worked. There was no reaching Karen with
reason, and she did not seem to care whether she was
treated with sympathy or not. She did not seem bothered by
what had happened, nor apprehensive about what might
happen next.

"What's the minister at your chapel going to say about
making a pact with the Devil?"

"We didn't make a pact with the Devil."

"Karen, there are descriptions in all four of your diaries."

"We only pretended to. It was only like acting a play."

"What was going to happen in the next act, Karen?"

"I don't know what you mean."

"You played at putting yourself in league with the Devil.
What were you going to play at getting him to do for you?"

"We stopped playing the game. We couldn't think of
anything else. It got boring."

"Is there any point in all this?" Karen's mother asked.

Polly Parrott tried another tack. She read aloud one of
Davina's Rabelaisian descriptions of the morals of the
Parbold parents in which Karen was said to have concurred
with every word. It was offensive material, and she expected an explosion from Mrs. Parbold. But it came in an
unexpected form.

"Sergeant Parrott, we have gone over all this at home.
That was one of the reasons why my husband destroyed
Karen's diaries."

There remained the entry in Karen's current diary about
the telephone call that her father had had from Henry Gower
an hour before he was killed. Kenworthy had insisted that
she was not to mention this. He had said it was a devastating
weapon, but once it had been fired, it could not be fired
again. To reveal it before they had back-up for it was to
waste it.

Polly Parrott came away with a sick feeling of failure—

and the conviction that she had given Patsy Price a sorry tale for the lower reaches of the Norfolk CID to relish.

Again Hannah Maslin appeared in public in the afternoon. Unlike yesterday, she took no pains to hide either her progress or her objective. She went to the home of the asthmatic Linda Calvert, two of whose back bedroom windows overlooked the Parbolds' garden.

She was in there a good half-hour, and when she came out, Linda Calvert showed her to her garden gate, conversing happily.

Kenworthy waited until school was out before making himself known to Mrs. Ellis. She was a bonny, bespectacled woman, Welsh, benign and a non-stop talker. Kenworthy wondered how a man could cope with such an assault at breakfast-time.

"Is there anything special I can tell you, Mr. Kenworthy? I seem to have answered so many questions, to so many people."

"You must be wondering if you'll ever get the school back to normal."

"It will never be what it was. But I'm not sure that that's the same thing as normal. I don't say we were an outstanding school, but in a lot of ways we were an unusual one."

"Henry Gower was clearly a rare spirit."

"I like to think that he and I complemented each other. We did not always see eye to eye. But if I was doing something he disagreed with, he rarely interfered. He always said that the only things that worked were the ones people believed in."

"So what did you not see eye to eye with him about?"

"His judgements—of people and some children."

"Children like Davina Norris?"

"He got exasperated with Davina sometimes."

"And you didn't?"

"More often than he did. But as a teacher that's nothing

to be proud of. Davina's background was disturbed and disturbing."

"Yes. I can see that the troubles in her life are not simple. And I don't see how she's going to find her way out of them. But you were telling my Sergeant Parrott yesterday that Davina was not really the leader of the famous four."

"I am sure she is not. Davina is a great doer of things—but not an initiator: an executive, not a policy-maker. She sometimes persuades people to do things. But she's not what I'd call a compeller."

"And you think Karen Parbold is?"

"Karen Parbold is a difficult child to understand. She is insidious. She is deep. And to my mind she is by far the cleverest of the four."

"The Blouet IQ scores don't support that."

"An IQ isn't the last word. And Karen seldom extends herself. Once she sees she's going to pass, she slackens off. She's not interested in high-flying. In old fashioned language, she's lazy. I've known her cheat in a school examination—not because she found it difficult, but to save herself effort."

"It still surprises me to hear you say she influences the others. She doesn't strike me as being an attractive personality."

"I don't say she is. She's sly. She thinks of things seconds, minutes—sometimes days—before others do. She has an acid tongue. She can raise laughs at other people's expense. She has a natural command of ridicule. Her friends are afraid of being dropped from her good books. And those who aren't in them stand little chance of being admitted."

"Tell me something about her background."

"Repressive—oh, from the best of motives—but she is a twentieth-century child, and her parents are barely twentieth-century people. The chapel community in this village is a small one, close-knit. They keep a sharp lookout for each other's transgressions. They are soaked through and through with that old strain of English puritanism that looks on pleasure as a mortal danger. I don't know whether Karen has knowingly rejected their creed yet—it's probably a little early for that. But she certainly knows what it is to suffer from it."

The classroom was a busy one: its walls were a record of enthusiasms: from intergalactic rocket-liners to posters of field grasses.

"I'm not saying that Mr. Parbold is a bad man, Mr. Kenworthy. By his own and his friends' lights, I'm sure he's a good one. But he's difficult. I've heard him argue that there can only be one total at the bottom of a column of figures—and likewise only one solution to any problem he comes up against. Karen lives subject to rigid discipline. Sometimes she is harshly punished, usually by being deprived of some treat. And once a thing is decreed, there is no relenting in that house."

"I suppose it has not helped, his being out of work?"

"No. And since he is only partially qualified, he knows he may not find himself back at a desk again in a hurry. It has made him very sour. But this business with Henry Gower has put the finishing touch to his disillusionment. They were good friends, Nigel and Henry: opposites, perhaps, but they got something out of being opposites. But when the girls brought these charges, it was final, as far as Nigel Parbold was concerned."

"From firm friends to bitter enemies."

"I'm sure that Henry did not look on Nigel as an enemy. But the other way round—!"

But a man wouldn't kill another for indecent behaviour, would he? Even against his own daughter? Or might he?

· 19 ·

TOM WILSON HAD requisitioned a portable foreman's office to give Kenworthy at least an impression of privacy. His first client after the partitions had been erected was Linda Calvert, pushing in Gemma in her buggy. She was breathless to tell an ill-organized story. Hannah Maslin, it seemed, had come to her house wheezing, but for once with good will.

"She said she had been thinking again about my offer to gather herbs for her. She had scrawled a list of things I could get from a herbalist that she would make up for my asthma. I wondered what had happened to make her change heart—well, she couldn't hide it. She wanted to ask me something about Nigel Parbold—you know that our garden overlooks his?"

What Mrs. Maslin wanted to know was whether she had ever seen Parbold wearing a cowboy hat like Sheriff Thurlow's.

"I had to think hard. I almost told her No. But then I remembered that sometimes when he's mowing on a hot summer's day, or lounging in a deckchair, I've seen him in an old wide-brimmed straw thing just like a cowboy's."

She stopped talking because Kenworthy was gazing fixedly ahead of himself with a peculiar expression, and she thought he was not listening. Then she followed the line of his gaze. He was looking at the hat that had blown across Mill Lane, now hanging on one of his office pegs.

"It was very like that one," Linda Calvert said.

"And what did Mrs. Maslin say, when you told her?"

"She said I was to come straight and tell you. I suppose she wouldn't come herself because every few yards are a torture to her."

"No. She wouldn't come herself because she has decided to be helpful—but doesn't want it to look that way."

Davina Norris was coming down through the village as Hannah Maslin was half way home. She fell in step with her, and they went into the cottage together. One of Wilson's sleuths reported this at the Centre immediately.

Detective-Superintendent Arnold Blane drove unheralded and casually into St. Botolph's just as an artificially blonde twelve-year-old was coming out of one of the older cottages carrying an obviously heavy brown paper parcel. The detective-constable who had been watching Hannah Maslin offered to carry it for her. But she refused adamantly to allow it out of her hands. She took it to the Report Centre and asked to see Kenworthy. But Kenworthy was not in. He and Sergeant Parrott were in the Parbold home, talking to Nigel Parbold.

Parbold's hands started shaking when he opened his door and saw Kenworthy holding his straw Stetson. But as Kenworthy said to Polly in his later analysis, there are other things that a man can be guilty of besides murder. Bloody stupidity, for one; and for another, trying to lean on a cover story that is too flimsy and too complex.

"I'm afraid, Chief Inspector—"

"Are you, now?"

This time there was no difficulty about being admitted. Parbold was anxious to get the couple into his house and out of sight of St. Botolph's.

"When I say I'm afraid, I mean I don't know how I'm going to make you believe this."

"Try."

"It's hard to know where to start."

"Anywhere you like, Parbold. We'll put it together in

some sort of order when you've finished. Perhaps a good opening line would be the telephone call you had from Henry Gower the night the poor devil was killed."

"You know about that?"

"And I'm never going to tell you how I know."

"Gower and I were the best of friends, until—Honestly, Chief Inspector, I had to believe that he was guilty. I'm still shocked beyond description that Karen could have been a party to inventing the story they told. It was so intricate and thorough."

"The court would probably have made the same mistake," Kenworthy said with devastating quietness. "We were talking about a telephone call."

"Gower and I had been the best of friends, always at each other's house. I took it badly. He'd tried before to get me to listen to him—I didn't want to know. Of all those determined to ruin him, I was the most voluble. But when he rang me the night before last, there was something in his voice that made me think twice. I changed my mind. I changed my mind, Mr. Kenworthy, because there was an honesty in his despair that even I could not reject out of hand. Henry, you know, was almost too honest to live in a dishonest world."

Parbold was grey and shadow-cheeked. His was the face of a man whose several worlds had crashed. It was the face of a religious man whose child had been proven a monstrous liar, her mind declared a pit of filth.

Kenworthy kept the ludicrous hat prominently on his knee.

"Henry admitted to me on the phone," Parbold said, "that he had tried to waylay Elsie Frost after school, in full view of all the mothers. He had approached Davina and walked a few yards with her, but had not been able to make an impression. He knew that he had left himself vulnerable. He had broken the conditions of his bail. It was only a matter of time before they pulled him in. But he had a little time. There is a chronic shortage of patrol cars in this police district and a network of lanes that they could not search all at once. He cycled to Ingwold St. Clements, phoned me from a kiosk, pleaded with me to meet him in the engine-house; persuaded me. I put on the hat—one I bought years ago on the Costa del Sol. I left it till the light was failing, didn't want to be seen going anywhere, least of all to the pumphouse. I claim no originality for aping Thurlow. More than one married man in St. Botolph's has got to places where he wouldn't care to be found by being mistaken for the Sheriff in bad light at a distance."

"But you didn't get to the pumphouse? Did you get to speak to Henry Gower?"

"No. As I came in sight of Hannah Maslin's, I saw Davina come out of her gate. She must have caught sight of Henry at the same moment as I did, entering the village along the road from Back Fen. Davina dodged into Mill Lane and I followed. Then I knew from tyres behind me that Henry had seen her."

"You caught up with her?"

"No. She was forty yards in front and by the time I had turned the corner, she was nowhere in sight. She could have taken cover in a ditch on either side of the lane. I scrambled down the bank on my left. She must have chosen the other side, gaining further advantage. I didn't find her. Henry put on a spurt, shouted something I didn't catch and went on ahead. But he was wasting his time, going after her. The lane is straight, along that stretch. There was a car coming behind us with its headlamps on full beam, and if Davina had been on the road, we could not have missed seeing her. I was certain she could not be far away. I crossed the road to look in the other ditch. Then my silly hat blew off. I tried to chase it. It was absurd what one will try to do at critical moments. I spent a long time looking for Davina. Her safety seemed more important than keeping Henry waiting. I spent three-quarters of an hour looking for her, calling her name. Finally I gave up, went along the sea-wall to the engine-house: no sign of Henry. By the time I was back in the village, Henry's body had been found and the hue and cry was on."

Parbold breathed out heavily.

"I don't expect you to believe a word of this."

Kenworthy was unexpectedly testy.

"How can I believe anything until I know more—or disbelieve it either?"

Davina was waiting patiently in the village hall, clutching her brown paper parcel. When Kenworthy returned with Sergeant Parrott, he called her at once into his foreman's office.

"I've come to bring you something, and to explain something," she said. "Mr. Kenworthy, they won't send me to the sort of place that Sergeant Parrott was talking about, will they?"

"That's not in my hands. I wouldn't think it at all unlikely."

"Mr. Kenworthy, if I give you this—I know it's tremendously important—if I tell you something—will it help me not to be sent away?"

"No deals, Davina," he said. "And I'd say that to bigger game than you."

Sergeant Parrott got up suddenly, came round the desk, snatched the parcel and tore it open. Davina protested furiously—which Kenworthy and the sergeant exacerbated by laughing. The package contained ledgers, a box-file and various bank passbooks.

"What are these?" Kenworthy asked, in the tone of a man who did not propose to be messed about. Davina was wise enough to see that she had better control herself.

"My father keeps them at home in a wall-safe. I found the combination because my mother hasn't the brains to remember it, and keeps it written down. I've heard him talk to Mummy about his private accounts. I don't know anything about them, but I do know that he keeps them at home because he daren't have them in his office. Sometimes in the evening, when he's at home, he works at them, but I'm not allowed to be in the same room when he does."

Kenworthy turned a page or two.

"Yes. I think I know what these are. Thank you very much, Davina—but they don't buy you anything."

"But I haven't brought them to try to do a deal, Mr. Kenworthy. I decided a week or two ago that I was going to show these to someone who mattered. That was what I meant when I wrote that I was going to do something real. I know it's not bad the way you look at it. But I was going to give my father away—it's all he deserves—and that's a bad thing for a daughter to do, isn't it? So I took them down, a few at a time, to Mrs. Maslin's for safe-keeping."

"Davina, I want a full account of your movements the night Mr. Gower was killed."

Either she knew that they had her where they wanted her, or she was inventing with fluent gaiety as she answered.

"Well, I'd been to Mrs. Maslin's with the last of these books. Just as I came out, to come home, I saw Mr. Gower in front of me and there was someone else behind me. It was that mad cowboy man. I turned into Mill Lane to try to get away from both of them and jumped the ditch at the bottom of the sea-wall. It isn't a sea-wall nowadays, of course, and I knew where there was a little tunnel through it, something to do with the land-drains. It was filthy, wet and smelly, but I hid in there, and heard Karen's father calling my name and go stampeding all over the place. I stayed where I was until he went away. The entrance to my little archway was hidden behind bulrushes, and if you didn't know it was there, you'd only find it by accident."

"And when you came out?"

"I climbed the bank to the sea-wall, and heard horrible sounds not far off. I know now that it must have been two men fighting in the field. I started to run away, then I heard one of the men scream hideously. I went on running, fell down, got up again. Then there was somebody else along the lane, I don't know who. There were cars on the road. There was a man on the road, searching everywhere. I know now that it was one of your detectives. I tried to run away from him. I fell into a reed-bed—you do believe this, don't you, Mr. Kenworthy?"

"Some of it."

Sergeant Parrott inserted herself into the dialogue.

"I don't believe a word she's said."

"No?" Kenworthy asked pleasantly.

"Davina—when you wrote in your diary about something real, you didn't mean your father's accounts. When you spirited them away from the house, it wasn't to hand them over to authority. It was to threaten to, perhaps—to scare your father out of his wits. We call that blackmail. But what you meant by real was that the doctors found out about you yesterday morning. Chief Inspector, do you think that Davina and I might have a little talk together on our own?"

"By all means," Kenworthy said, and Davina could see his eyes twinkling. But there was no light in Davina's eyes. Perhaps she had thought that Kenworthy was easy meat. But she clearly did not relish this woman sergeant.

·20·

KENWORTHY DID NOT know where Sergeant Parrott had taken Davina for their essentially feminine chat, but they were away a long time. He sat and tried to make out a basic pattern in Norris's personal accounts.

He did not profess expertise on company fraud. There were things here that meant nothing to him, but the need for secret records on this scale, dangerous though they were, was at once apparent. Norris's dealings and diversifications were too complex to be entrusted to memory. Here, for disentanglement by the backroom buffs, were Norris's encoded reserves and stashings away, holding companies untraceable to him, his money-laundering systems, an overall balance reaching at the end of today into six columns of figures. Kenworthy did not know the exact date of the failure of the Basildon mail order concern, but there were transfers at about that time that had clearly been concealed from the receiver. That falsification alone was enough to put him inside for an effective spell. There was no wonder that Cynthia Norris had been vague and nervous on the subject of a search warrant, the first time Kenworthy had entered her home. Doubtless it had been impressed on her to the point of boredom that there were documents of indescribable delicacy on the premises—and that her own continuing solvency depended on them.

From within the green-panelled security of his foreman's office, Kenworthy was aware of someone's noisy entrance into the village hall. The duty sergeant appeared, attempting to usher in a man who was already getting ahead of him: a large, self-confident man, who a decade and a half ago might have been considered good-looking by some; a well-fed-and-wined man with a contempt for those about him and their petty opinions; a very angry man. Kenworthy had not seen a portrait of Norris, but there was nothing ambiguous about the way this man's attention was homing in on the small stack of accounts books that were the sole content of Kenworthy's desk.

"Are you Kenworthy? You have no right whatever to enter a man's home—"

"I have never entered your home except at your wife's invitation."

"And as for taking away private papers—"

"The only private papers I came away with belong to your daughter."

"I shall see you broken for this, Kenworthy."

Did Norris not know that the damage must surely already be done? Or was he capable of carrying on a bluff until the final slamming of the metal door?

"Sit down, Mr. Norris."

Kenworthy pushed the pile of books toward Norris with his knuckles.

"I'm afraid this sort of thing means very little to me. These came into my possession through no initiative of mine. I apologize for any inconvenience—"

Norris sank into the chair opposite Kenworthy's, hardly able to believe his ears—but also unable to resist the temptation of the moment.

"Say what you like, Kenworthy—this will go further."

"When did you get back from Java?" Kenworthy asked amiably.

"Last leg this morning. Flew in from Amsterdam."

"I'll be wanting to see your passport," Kenworthy said. "And the sooner I can see it, the sooner we can eliminate an unlikely possibility."

"Oh, come off it, Chief Inspector—"

"Shall we go up to your house together now?"

"Really, Mr. Kenworthy—" and Norris laughed, the laughter of a man of this world who pities small-minded conventions.

"You'll find the Amsterdam rubber stamp, Kenworthy—and one from Ibiza. You don't really think I've been charging about the China Seas, do you?"

"I'd wondered," Kenworthy said blandly.

"I take it you can be discreet, Kenworthy. My dear wife only gets upset over what she knows about."

"Just for the form, I'd still better see your passport. I'll bring these accounts with me to your house."

"That's all right. I'll take them. Let me drive you."

"I'll bring my car. I'm going elsewhere afterwards. I'll follow you up."

Kenworthy picked up the books. Whose bluff would win? Norris's aggression or Kenworthy's mildness? Norris did not want to stir Kenworthy's suspicions—and there were a lot of Kenworthy's policemen in the hall. Kenworthy let Norris precede him—thus affording himself the opportunity for a rapid-fire briefing of CI Tom Wilson.

"Tom, there are two things I want done in next to no time."

Wilson was the sort who did not need to be told things twice—nor to have his priorities underscored.

"Find out where in England Norris spent last night and the night before—probably a hotel in East Anglia, and he won't have used his own name. But if there's a column in the hotel register for his car number, he'll have entered the correct one. He's the sort for whom a car's a car, especially when it's a Merc. Or he may have hired one."

Wilson saw nothing to question in any of that.

As Kenworthy was following Norris's car out of the hall grounds, he saw Polly Parrott coming back with Davina. They appeared to be on terms of laughing friendship.

The next thing had to be the reconstruction. Perhaps it seemed unrealistic to do it by daylight, but it did enable them to see more of their surroundings than the principals the other night could have done. Davina was being played by Patsy Price. DC Warburton, on a bicycle, was Henry Gower. Kenworthy, taking childish pleasure in wearing the straw Stetson, was Nigel Parbold. Connie Kimble, driving a police car, was waiting in the village with her eye on a stopwatch. They had settled times and distances with great precision.

Patsy Price came out of Hannah Maslin's gate. Kenworthy, pretending to walk like John Wayne, came down the village street behind her and turned the corner into Mill Lane. By the time she had rounded the angle, she was out of his sight, having made a dash for the drainage conduit where Davina said she had hidden.

Kenworthy scrambled down into the ditch on his left, as Parbold had described his own actions. Connie turned into Mill Lane in a pale blue Escort. Parbold had said that the car had had its beam full on, and that the road ahead had shown no sign of Davina. The car drove on. DC Warburton entered the lane on his bicycle, shouting something indistinguishable to Kenworthy as he passed him.

So far they had followed Parbold's narrative meticulously. Now came the experiment. Warburton got off his bicycle by a gate giving access to the sea-wall, this being the route that Gower would have followed to get himself to the engine-house. Connie in her car was abreast of him as he manhandled his machine. She drove on a hundred yards, pulled up, got herself surprisingly athletically across the ditch, scrambled up the bank, waited for Warburton to reach her, leaped up at him and kicked his rear wheel, breaking a couple of spokes. The detective-constable fell off, and they seized each other's wrists as symbol of a wrestling bout that they did not allow to develop.

Kenworthy put his hand in his pocket, drew out a referee's whistle and blew a hard blast, making the conventional infantryman's signal for his troops to converge on him.

"Yes. It's possible," he said.

* * *

Norris, Tom Wilson reported, had indeed hired a car,
leaving his own at the airport, where it had stood since he
had first gone away. He had spent only the first night, the
night of the murder, in England—in a motel between King's
Lynn and Swaffham. He had signed in as John
Braybrooke—but as Kenworthy had forecast, had entered
the correct registration number of the hired car.

On the second night, he appeared to have vanished
without trace. But this time the hired car as well as his own
had remained parked overnight at Norwich Airport, and he
flew in from Amsterdam the next morning. It was not yet
clear how he had achieved this, but it could easily have been
managed by travelling to Harwich and crossing into Holland
on the night boat.

Forensic made two interesting discoveries in the interior
of the car that Norris had driven. There was alluvial mud on
the carpet and pedals identifiable as possibly from the
sea-wall and the pastures beyond it; also algæ similar to
specimens to be found in the culvert from which Norman
Purkis had dragged Gower's body.

There remained the desirability of finding the murder
weapon, which had still not come to light after Norris had
been remanded in custody from his committal proceedings.
Arnold Blane kept reminding all patrols to be on the lookout
for this, but it was two schoolboys who eventually brought
in something that they had found in a ditch between King's
Lynn and Swaffham, where it could have been thrown from
the window of a car. It was a pocket-sized flick-knife—the
sort that might be carried by a man anxious to prove his
macho—to himself if not to others.

"Well, come on, Polly. Let's have the disgusting truth,"
Kenworthy had said, when he saw her after his first talk to
Norris.

"Well, actually, you put me on to it yourself," she told
him.

"I'm always doing that sort of thing for junior colleagues. What oil have I struck this time?"

"You said that anything that Davina knew about sex she had learned from books she had found about the house. Well, books aren't the only thing in the Norris home. You also once asked me my opinion on Cynthia as a sex kitten. Less than a contented cow, it appears. Among her possessions—and Davina found it—is a device known as a vibrator. It's a simulation, sir, of—"

"Yes. I know. I've seen one in a sex shop window. That's when my inferiority complex dates from."

"Davina was scared to use it at first, but determined to. More real than real, you might say."

"It must have been a traumatic experience."

"It was. Karen Parbold operated on her with it."

It was Norris's habit to return from his jaunts abroad suddenly and without announcement, sometimes entering the house stealthily in the middle of the night, as if he was expecting to find his wife in midstream adultery.

Many English travellers feel news-starved when they come home from long absences. Whether or not he had seen any recent English newspapers in Ibiza, he would almost certainly have made a bee-line for the latest edition as soon as he was on home soil. A recent edition even had a fudged picture of his daughter being escorted across the village carrying a bundle that might have worried him very much indeed. The evening he came home he found his wife drink-fuddled, Davina not to be found—and his accounts missing.

He did not ring her friends because he did not want to advertise his presence in St. Botolph's. No one in the village came forward to say he had seen Norris; but might not that be precisely why he had hired an inconspicuous car? Norris drove out to look for Davina, saw her come out of Hannah Maslin's, saw Gower follow her into Mill Lane—as also did that Sheriff idiot. Then he saw Henry Gower on his cycle, saw Gower mount the sea-wall, in a flush of sentiment hated Henry Gower for what he had done to his little girl, was convinced that Gower could only be near her in this spot at this hour with untowards intent.

Norris drove past Gower, got out of his car, climbed the bank as Connie Kimble had done, kicked the schoolmaster off his cycle. And Gower, thinking Norris was going to kill him, defended himself vigorously. In the fight that followed, the knife was flicked out and he was killed. Norris dragged his body to where it might take longer to find it.

That was the schema with which the Yard's solicitor briefed prosecuting silk. But it was not one of those neat cases in which the accused admitted himself cornered and gave everyone the satisfaction of a confession. Norris denied everything, at every stage, in the minutest detail. His brief made great play with the unreliability of forensic evidence found in a rented car. The jury had to be put up in a hotel, and twice came back to his Lordship for guidance. They were a shrewd, careful and convinced jury, bringing in a unanimous *guilty* verdict. Norris was put away for life, from which he gains occasional respite when he is brought out to help to confuse the issue about accounts which the Fraud Squad still hope will one day figure in a prosecution.

After the trail, Arnold Blane took Inspector Kimble on one side.

"A clever lot, these Londoners. But they wouldn't have done it without us."

Connie glowed sufficiently to say precisely the same words to WPC Price, who wrote them down on a piece of paper which she pinned to her bedsit wall.

A day or two after Norris had gone down, the Parbolds' chapel celebrated its Harvest Thanksgiving. For the first time, they felt like a family again. Pauline Dean has given up keeping a diary. Elsie Frost's parents wanted to decline the grammar school place that she won, but Gwynneth Ellis called at their home and (volubly) dissuaded them. Karen Parbold also won a High School place, but had not made any friends there by the middle of the first term.

Davina succeeded in charming all the social workers who flocked to see her. Her mother went into a private clinic for drying out—not for the first time in her life. While she was away, Davina went to an aunt in the shires, where she appears to have behaved circumspectly. She has not been to see Hannah Maslin again.

The one who has gained most from the upheaval in St. Botolph's Fen End is Linda Calvert, whose asthma is very much better now. She is making the most of the fruitful autumn, and almost daily brings old Hannah treasures from the fields, woods and marshes.